THE OLIVE TREE

THE OLIVE TREE

Mariam El Houli

First published in 2022 by Dean Publishing
PO Box 119
Mt. Macedon, Victoria, 3441
Australia
deanpublishing.com

Cataloguing-in-Publication Data
National Library of Australia
Title: The Olive Tree
Edition: 1st edn
ISBN: 978-1-92545-248-8
Category: Young Adult Fiction/Social Themes/Prejudice & Racism

DEDICATION

In loving memory of A Houli,
always loved and never forgotten.

To my mother, the queen of my heart.

To Suzanne Allan, not my sister by blood,
but my sister by choice. You were there from the start!

A NOTE ON READING

The Olive Tree is a work of fiction. Though *The Olive Tree* references real locations and historical events, it has limited factual basis. Geography, scenery, and certain contextual realities have been altered to assist the story. Certain locations within *The Olive Tree* have been completely fictionalised, though may bear similarities to actual places. Any opinions expressed are those of the characters and are not to be confused with the author's.

CONTENTS

CHAPTER 1

The years had taken their toll on the tree's once shining leaves. It stood lonely in the dark, branches hollow and drooping sadly in the breeze. Dull and hardened, deep cuts coiled up its trunk – an angry mess of slashes. Disease had spread through its roots, a tangling death that suffocated it slowly and painfully.

Many people had died pretending to own it. No one really did, of course; it had been there since before them all. That is what my mother told me every chance she could. It was the same old story that her mother had told her when she was young: *The Olive Tree*. My mother would make my grandmother recite it every night when she was little, each version altered slightly from the last.

"Once upon a time," she would say, "before the children of Adam set foot onto earth, the olive tree stood tall and unwavering, never bowing to the wind no matter how strong it blew. Its leaves leathery and lance shaped, they paired opposite one another on thin twigs that bore bitter and hard fruit. When the sons of Adam settled on earth, God elevated the status of the olive tree, declaring it a symbol of those who believed.

"The olive tree did not need much – not food nor water – to survive. Yet, it grew strong and robust – a symbol of great steadfastness for the sons of Adam. The olive tree was more than just a plant, transcending into a great icon of peace, resilience and light. Where it could, the tree offered the people sustenance, providing food for their families and work for their men."

I never understood why this was the only story that was ever told.

2017, Qu'laif, Israel
— though to the people, it will always be Palestine

Flanked by the sea to the west and the mountains to the east, our modest town of Qu'laif was a place like no other. From the lips of the Mediterranean, the sloping land sprawled far and long from the clear sapphire waters — the affluence of city dwellers' high-rise apartments and Euro vacationers' whitewashed villas eventually giving way to the crumbling facades of the neighbourhood that I called home. Winding up the mountain, the greenery grew grey, replaced by the cracked pathways and cobblestoned lanes that meandered through Qu'laif's throngs of low rent housing, dilapidated market stalls, and makeshift coffee shops. The smell of salt and sea fading into city pong, Qu'laif was a town of gritty charm — a hub of endurance, resilience, and grind.

Though the world saw Qu'laif as Israel, we did not. To us, it was rightfully Palestine — a land that had been taken, renamed and cleansed of its people. As Palestinians, we did not exist. We were simply blips on the Jewish State.

Despite this, Qu'laif was not a terrible place to be. We were safe — relatively speaking. Sure, the rumble of a shell detonating in the east, or the piercing cry of a neighbour's letterbox being torn apart by a makeshift grenade, rattled our house every now and then but never caused any real concern. After decades of unrest, we were used to it. What we lacked in safe streets, pretty parks and luscious lawns, we made up for in strength and stamina. We were a tough people, an indestructible people. We had to be.

Our humble neighbourhood was a melting pot of religions. Jews, Christians, Muslims, Ahmadiyya, and Druze lived and worked together. Compared to the majority of Palestinians and Israelis, we managed to co-exist somewhat peacefully, though the tension between 'us' and 'them' still suffocated every and any interaction. We all felt the pressure of cohabitation: like a plastic film had been stretched from one end of Qu'laif to the other – taught and tight and rippling with pull. 'You only mix with your own kind' was a rule that we all lived by. Our social bounds were defined, practised, and – when it came to my mother – enforced.

Nothing seemed to set my mother, Nada – a proud Islamic woman – off more than comingling with the Jewish 'settlers'. In fact, she forbade me from speaking to, or approaching, them at all.

"You mustn't look at them. Don't even *blink* in their direction," she'd whispered to me from the time I was small, making me fearful to even breathe the same air in case it was somehow contaminated. She behaved like we were antelope, and our neighbours vicious, hungry lions.

From what I could tell, this trope was not unique to my mother, or our religion. It seemed to be trotted out by every adult against anyone whose belief was not congruent with their own. This contempt was the undercurrent of my – and I imagine almost every other Qu'laifian kid's – upbringing. According to Mum, the Israelis were fascist Zionists who had stolen our homes and murdered our people (and wanted to continue doing so); and to the Zionists, we were terrorists who had not only established ourselves on land that was rightfully theirs, but were violent thugs that needed to be cleansed. We could not accept a Jewish State of Israel, just as they could not accept Arabs and Jews living in equality under a secular government, or allow Palestinians to exist within a State of their own, free of occupation. There was no empathy, no room for compromise.

It wasn't until I was 16 that I began to actively question why life was like this. If we all believed that the 'other side' was to blame for our unhappiness, didn't it make sense to accept that there may actually be two points of reasoning – however invalid we believed the other to be? Could it be that we had inherited our predecessors' prejudices, without actually considering whether there was a better way forward? Why was it that we continued down this path of conflict when the consequences were so dire? It seemed to me that it was more important to find any sort of peace and cohesion, even if it meant negotiation and concession.

I knew there was a lot I did not understand – perhaps I was too naïve, too sheltered from the realities of the past. But, deep down, I knew there had to be a way forward, to bridge the conflict between Palestinians and Israelis. Surely I wasn't the only one who felt frustrated by the constant barrage of hatred that underpinned the Palestinian existence. If knowledge and compassion were the antidote to prejudice, then I wanted to be as open-minded as I possibly could.

So, I could not accept my mother's caution. Contrary to what she thought, I believed that no human bore the sins of another – God created us equally. Of course, I did not dare tell her that.

One morning around the middle of September, I left for school. My baggy dress ballooned in the breeze, catching the wind as I stepped out onto the pave. The early sun already bright and bursting overhead, I turned my chin to the sky, bathing in warmth.

I attended a 'cocktail school', as I had coined it – a mixture of all ages and religions thrown together in a building that if you sneezed hard enough could collapse right on top of you. It serviced 1,000 students, yet there were only 20 classes. We would be packed in like sardines, most of the time lucky to find a corner in the classroom to squeeze into, rather than an actual seat to sit on. The kids who spoke Hebrew had a bit more luck – they were given their own classes and set of teachers, with only 20 students permitted per lesson. We all envied them. It was as if they attended their own private institution.

My younger brothers, Asmar and Fadi – the 'miracle twins', as I liked to call them – walked in front of me on their way to pre-primary. After my mother had me, she struggled to grow a baby again, and the doctors could not tell her why. Then, on her 47th birthday she vomited so much that we had to take her to hospital. It was only then that we found out she was pregnant with twins. Mum nearly passed out from shock, and my father clapped and jumped all through the ward.

I remember being completely overjoyed. I had always wanted a sibling to break my loneliness — a little play mate I could spend hours toying and fighting with. Now I'd be getting two! Looking back, the day Asmar and Fadi were born was one of the few times I had seen my mother truly happy.

"Stay on the pavement," I reminded Fadi as he skipped along, holding hands with his brother. "Be careful of cars."

As I glanced up, my eyes locked on Hannah on the other side of the street, no doubt also about to leave for school. With her long, black hair and big brown eyes, we could have been sisters — her tent dress draping well past her knees, almost as modest as mine. But there was one stark difference between us: she was a Jew, and I a Muslim. We could never be sisters; we couldn't even be friends.

Hannah and I had met many times before. In fact, some days we would stop near the school gate and chat briefly. We both spoke a little English, so could usually stumble our way through a conversation, despite the sneers that followed us.

"Hello," I greeted her.

Like most of the houses in Qu'laif, Hannah's was a simple stone box, wedged between a long line of others just like it. Though my dad had made improvements to our home where he could – mending the busted handrail that coiled its way up the stairs from the street to our front door, eradicating the weeds that shot up through the sidewalk's cracked cement – it seemed that Hannah's had largely left theirs to the wayside. Tinged yellow by years of neglect, Hannah's house looked more egg yolk than shell – its cream façade caked in a thick layer of grime. Two square windows, masked by thick, dark drapes, framed the front door.

Hannah smiled, nodding as she raised her hand to wave.

Then I saw movement in her house. The curtains fluttered and the door swung open with the force of a hurricane.

Her mother ran out, anger twisting her face. She grabbed Hannah by the wrist, screaming something at her in Hebrew. Asmar and Fadi froze at the sight, looking fearfully up at me as my stomach twisted.

We all gasped when Hannah's mother slapped her hard on the cheek, snapping her head to the side. Hot tears sprung to my eyes. I didn't want to see her hurt. "Come on," I muttered to my brothers as Hannah's mum came flying towards us like a bird of prey.

She yelled something I didn't understand and spat on the concrete at our feet. Shock and disgust rippled through me.

Poor Hannah. Her cheek was flaming red. She hung her head, a curtain of curls obscuring the rest of her face. As we watched on, footsteps sounded behind me. I didn't have to look to know it was Mother.

They stared at each other, my mum and Hannah's, looking one another up and down in disgust while their embarrassed and frightened children stood in between. I wanted to say something to break the silence, but no sound would come out, like my vocal chords had frozen in fear, too.

I winced when Mum grabbed me by the ear with one hand, my hair with the other, dragging me home. Her hijab fluttered in the breeze, loose hair shooting out beneath the thick chiffon. She had obviously thrown it on in a hurry.

"How many times have I told you that we don't talk to scumbag, Zionist child killers?" She shrieked like a banshee, her voice echoing up and down the street. I bet every neighbour from our street to Tel Aviv could hear her screaming and my howling. My twin brothers sloped after us in terrified silence.

I wanted to say that Hannah seemed like a perfectly nice girl, and I never saw her kill anyone, but all I could do was cry out as my scalp burned and my ear felt like it was going to be ripped from my head. Of all the times I'd seen my mother angry, this was one of the worst. As we were dragged back home, a scene from the Disney movie *The Lion King II: Simba's Pride* came to mind. Simba takes his daughter away from the 'outsiders'. I felt like that lost lion cub now, confused and angry that I was not allowed to talk to people because we were different.

I was not going to hear the end of this, and neither was Hannah. In another life, we may have been best friends. Hannah had told me that her parents were always fighting. She was an only child, and her father was a heavy drinker. Sometimes he got into fights with people on the streets, and Hannah and her mother would spend the nights crying.

My heart broke for her.

I had told her about my mum, my dad, Salim, and my grandma, Nazik. She giggled when I told her how the twins were always playing tricks on me, saying she wished she had a baby brother. I told her she would scrap that idea straight away if she spent just one day with Asmar and Fadi. We both laughed.

Mother gave me an earful as I scrubbed the kitchen floors as punishment – apparently, I would bring shame to the family, no one would want to marry a Zionist sympathiser, and I was going to get killed by a Jewish settler if I continued this behaviour. I rolled my eyes when she wasn't looking. You'd think that she'd caught me kissing a Jewish boy while drinking wine and reading from the Torah, the way she was carrying on. She'd ranted and raved so much over the years that I learnt some of her sayings off by heart. I longed to chant them with her, but all that would get me was a smack around the head and another week of chores.

I headed to my room, leaving my mother screaming after me. Grandma was sitting in the corner of the living room, knitting a hat for one of the boys. She nodded occasionally, agreeing with my mum. I resisted the urge to punch something on the way past. This time I'd been punished for an entire week, and each day of it was going to be hell. I wouldn't even be allowed to go to school, let alone watch TV. Even if the United Nations came to our doorstep and commanded she free me, she wouldn't budge.

My mum wasn't always like this. I had fond memories of her: of her reading books to me when I was a kid, of us cooking together. I remembered her hugs and the way she always smelled of violets. But there was something about me speaking to Jewish people, including Hannah, that made her fly off the handle, like she suddenly transformed into a dragon with fire bursting from her nostrils.

I tried to ask her why once, but all she said to me was, "When you grow up, you'll understand." Well, I was 16 now, and I wasn't any closer to getting it. What was there to understand? Why couldn't we be friends with our neighbours?

I collapsed onto my bed with a sigh, thinking miserably about the long week I'd have ahead of me, cleaning, studying and stripped of anything fun, simply for saying hello to a girl my own age. I started to doze off, my mother's voice echoing in my head. As I drifted in and out of sleep, her words ran round and round: "Nisma, don't talk to the child killers"; "Nisma, your sympathy toward the enemy is a betrayal of your people"; and her favourite thing to say, whenever I challenged her – "Nisma, opinions are a privilege for the rich, not the poor."

A soft creak from the floorboards outside interrupted my thoughts – it must have been the twins. I snapped my head up to snarl them away. I was not in the mood to play. But it was my father, talking to my mum. I rose from the bed as carefully as I could and tiptoed to my bedroom door.

"Salim, you have to do something about our daughter," said Mum. "She doesn't understand what she's doing. She just trusts everyone around her." As I peeked out from my room, I was shocked to see that my mother was crying. My heart gave an uncomfortable squeeze.

"Nada, take it easy," my father said, his voice soft as he gently ran his large hands up her arms. "She's just a child. You know how inquisitive she is."

"What's that supposed to mean?" Mum snapped. "I let her befriend the enemy? I let her do whatever she wants, and then I bury her with all the others?"

Confusion rippled through me. *Bury?*

My father remained silent. He didn't argue with her when she was angry. "I'll talk to her," he said, letting out a low sigh. "I'll make sure she doesn't talk to that girl again."

I stayed by the door, listening as he talked quietly to my grandmother about his day. Apparently, the Israeli soldiers were disputing some nearby olive trees.

"They want to cut them down to make room for new houses."

My heart ached at the sound of this. How could people be so cruel? To fell those ancient trees that provided a livelihood for so many.

Though I couldn't see him, I knew my dad was rubbing the bridge of his nose – a habit of his when anything upset him. We were all tired of the fighting.

"They have no hearts, Salim," my grandma croaked. "Be careful, my son, when you deal with them."

"Don't worry yourself, Mother. I know an Israeli soldier that will make sure no one comes near us. For a price."

The kettle rattled as he put it on to boil. Footsteps sounded towards my room and I quickly sat on my bed, snatching up the nearest textbook and opening it to a random page.

"Nisma," he called softly through my door. "Can I come in?"

"Yes, Daddy."

Dad looked more tired than usual. He seemed

older, somehow, as though the day had sapped his energy. His ginger beard was now almost white, bright against his golden skin.

"Nisma, your mother told me that you've been speaking to Hannah again," he said, his voice low as he perched on the edge of my bed. "How many times has she asked you not to do that?"

I set the textbook aside. "Dad, I only said hello to her. She's a nice girl, I swear. Why does Mum not like her? Why does she blow up so easily? Why do they hate us, and why are we supposed to hate them?"

Dad crossed his legs. "Nisma, you need to understand that your mother loves you. We both do. She's worried about you. We're in a state of war with the Israelis who've occupied our land, taken away our livelihoods by destroying our crops, killed and imprisoned our people. And you still want to be friends with them? Didn't you see what they did in Gaza? Even our holy mosque Al-Aqsa is under siege."

"But not all of them are the same," I said in earnest. "Some of them are normal people. They want to live in peace, go to school, raise a family, just like you and me. They don't want bloodshed; they just want to be safe, like us. You can't judge someone just because of their religion or where they're from.

Why can't we judge people individually?"

Dad looked like he wanted to interrupt, but I continued. "Doesn't it say in The Qur'an that no person is responsible for another, and everyone will be judged *alone* by God on the Day of Judgement?"

Surprise painted my father's face. He paused, contemplative.

"When did you grow up, Nisma?" he finally said, his voice soft. "All that you said would be true if we were in a different country or under different circumstances. If the Israelis were… I don't know, *normal*, and lived under our flag, then yes, peace would be an option. Nisma, you need to understand that we're against Zionism, not Judaism. You're only 16. I don't want you to worry about these things now. You have grades. Don't upset or disobey your mother anymore, all right? She has your best interests at heart, even if you think otherwise. You won't understand how precious a child is until you have one yourself."

I nodded in acquiescence. My father was never going to understand. He planted a kiss on my forehead and closed my bedroom door behind him, leaving me alone and cross-legged on the sheets. I thought about what he said, but I couldn't agree with him.

As often is the case with debates, I only thought of points to make after he left. I wanted to ask where all the men had been when the Jewish settlers moved here in 1948. If it was something they were against, why didn't they stop them?

Last year, I asked our history teacher, Mr Yacoub, that very question. He stared at me like I'd sprouted an extra head, then barked at me to stand on one foot with my hands against the wall.

"What an insolent, unpatriotic question," he snarled as I lifted a foot, my cheeks burning with humiliation. "You're an unmannered girl. It's because of people like you that Palestine will never be free of occupation. Two weeks' detention!"

When I went home that day and told Mum what had happened, she said I probably deserved it. "I know you and the types of silly questions you'd ask at school," she said, shaking her head. "You embarrass yourself in front of everyone. Be thankful detention was all you got."

I sighed, collapsing back on the bed, the textbook's hard cover digging into my spine. Punished for asking a simple question.

I'd sleep on it. Next time I talked to my father, I'd ask him. Maybe he'd have a real answer for me.

CHAPTER 2

I woke the next day to the glaring sun hitting my eyes and the noise of my brothers bickering over a toy Mum had made them. I pulled a pillow over my face, groaning and wishing I could block out their crying. I wouldn't get any more sleep with that racket.

They were in the living room, tugging at the toy, tiny fists clasped around a sewn leg.

"It's mine!" screamed Fadi.

"No! It's mine, not yours!" yelled Asmar.

I marched over to them and yanked the toy out

of their little hands, holding it high so they couldn't reach it.

"Enough," I said sternly over their bawling. "Now, without fighting, who is the toy for?"

"Me!" they both screeched.

Though they were mid-tantrum, tears streaming down their red cheeks, their identical anguish made me laugh. They looked so cute, even when they were fighting. It wasn't easy getting the truth out of two angry toddlers.

"Well, let's ask Mum. We'll find out."

They trailed after me as I followed the smell of breakfast to the kitchen, where Mum was chopping tomatoes.

"Good morning," I said, knowing she wouldn't answer me. As I expected, she threw me an angry glance, her dicing turning vicious.

I pretended not to notice. I wouldn't give her the satisfaction.

"The boys are fighting over this little toy," I said, holding it up by the paw. It was somewhere between a bunny and a bear, and looking a little worse for wear after their fight. "Who is it for?"

"It's for them both," she replied shortly. "They're to share it without fighting or it'll be taken away. I told them that when I gave it to them."

"Did you hear that, boys?" I bellowed over my shoulder. "Now, either you share like good kids and play with it together, or neither of you can play with it. Deal?"

It wasn't a deal. They cried and stamped their feet and pummelled each other with angry little fists until finally, they agreed to share and play together nicely. They skipped off, holding one paw each, their fight forgotten. I watched them with a chuckle, wishing my mum could let go of her anger as easily.

Mum was whisking eggs with the tomatoes. I put the pan on the stove, passing her the salt. She avoided my gaze, whisking until the eggs became fluffy.

"Mum," I said softly. "I don't want us to fight. Why don't you ever hear me out? Can't we agree to disagree? I'm not a kid anymore, I'm 16. I wish we could get along."

She finally looked at me. The same expression I'd received from my teacher painted her face: pained confusion fused with acute indignation. I had turned to leave when she finally said, "Nisma, sit down, all right? I want to talk to you about something."

Surprised, I sat at the kitchen table. She cooked

the eggs in silence, then got out a handful of plates.

"First of all, nothing I say now will change the fact that you're grounded, as a lesson for what happened yesterday."

I wanted to roll my eyes, but focused on arranging my face as blankly as possible. "Yes, Mum."

I watched her empty the pan of scrambled eggs and tomatoes into a large serving dish. She placed the bowl of food down in front of me, before arranging five smaller plates around it. The runner on the table looked more like a jigsaw puzzle than a regular cloth, its tapestry a mismatch of colours and fabrics. Like almost all our belongings, it was a hand-me-down, a piece that had spent its life being restitched by many hands over many years, until it eventually found its way to our kitchen table.

On rare occasions where we could buy something new, we had to share it with the rest of the Muslim community in our neighbourhood. One time, Mum found a new pot on sale in the marketplace, and every lady on the street had to borrow it to make soup.

I asked my mum at the time, "Imagine if we'd never bought the pot. How would they have made any soup at all?"

She glared at me and said, "Don't be so selfish,

Nisma. They're not going to break it."

"I wasn't trying to be selfish," I had grumbled. "I was just asking a question. Is that such a crime?"

She covered the eggs with a cloth so they wouldn't get cold. I swallowed, wondering if I was in for the verbal beating of a lifetime. She sighed as she sank into the chair opposite me. "Nisma, I want you to understand that I love you and your brothers very much. No one and nothing is as precious as you. You might think that I don't understand you or even that I am against you, but that's not true. I just want what's best for you."

"But you never even give me a chance, Mum."

"Hear me out please, Nisma," she said. I thought that was a little hypocritical, but I shut my mouth and listened.

"I've never told you this before, but I think it's time," she said, leaning back. "When my father was a small boy, the Israelis invaded our country. They took our land, our identity, and our jobs — dispossessing and displacing hundreds of thousands of Palestinians and forcing many to seek asylum across the Arab world. Following the *Nakba*, my father's family fled, managing to settle in the east, where the State of Israel did not reach.

"My father and his family worked hard to

establish themselves, eventually building up a small shoemaking business in East Jerusalem. My dad met my mother and they eventually took over the shop from Dad's parents.

"Then, about a year before I was born, war knocked at our door again. The Israelis annexed Palestine and the Israeli occupation began. And so, the Palestinian people grew poorer and poorer – the autonomy to govern their own people all but removed. Eventually, my father's business collapsed – who wants to buy shoes for their children when they can't even afford a loaf of bread? When I was nine, I was pulled out of school and went to work for a bakery to help the family with money."

I cupped my face in my palms, resting my elbows on the table. I'd never heard this story before.

"Your grandmother cried for two weeks straight when I started working. I was their only child, and she wanted me to become a doctor, not a bakery worker. But we didn't have a choice. It was work or starve." She gave a bitter smile, lost in memories. I didn't interrupt her.

"Not one school was open. They were all either bombed or empty – parents refused to send their children there, fearing for their safety. I didn't understand what was going on at the time, really;

I thought we were having an extra-long holiday. Though the bakery was right next to our house, my mother checked on me every hour or so. The boss got irritated, but she'd beg and plead to him that I was her only child, that she just wanted to make sure I was safe. When the bell rang and she walked in, he didn't do much except shake his head.

"She couldn't work herself. She was born with only one arm and no one would hire her for jobs which usually required two. She was always self-conscious about it. I remember she'd wear big, long robes and dresses to hide it. But she never asked for help or complained about it, not once. I never saw her as different. My cousins sometimes talked about her behind her back, saying she was disabled. I always hated that. But my mother always had a smile on her face."

I thought about having to work in a bakery at nine years old. I imagined my mother as a small child, elbow-deep in flour.

"As time went on, the fighting got worse. Even the bakery had to close. Mother and I stayed at home while Father worked odd jobs, trying to make ends meet as best he could. Some nights we didn't eat much, and a lot of the time Father gave me his food, insisting that I needed it more." Her eyes grew glassy, and she blinked hard. I reached over and gently stroked her hand.

"My two uncles lived upstairs – your great uncles. At dinnertime, we'd eat together as one big family. Usually it was just bread or rice, but I always enjoyed those dinners when there was enough for us all to eat. After dinner, I'd play with my cousins. We'd tie each other's hair in ponytails and squabble over whose was best."

I listened carefully to each word, my mother grasping onto her memories like smoke. I'd never heard details of her childhood, only that, like everyone around us, life had been hard.

"When I was 11 years old, my mother sent me to her sister's house to stay. My aunt had more food than us as my uncle owned a piece of land that they lived off. They had a cow, two sheep, and a few hens. That might not sound like much, but back then she was considered very well off. We had eggs for breakfast in the mornings and milk to drink, too.

"I asked Mother to come with me, of course, but she wouldn't. She said that Father would never leave the house and that she wouldn't be a burden on anyone. 'I'll never leave his side,' she said. I remember her scent that day; she'd crushed some dry petals and scattered them among her dress. I gave her an extra-long hug and kissed my father. I'd never stayed at my aunt and uncle's house before, and I was nervous."

I could imagine. Eleven was still so young. I don't know what I would have done if I had had to live away from Mum and Dad as a kid, even if they did drive me crazy sometimes.

"That was the last time I ever saw my parents alive."

Tears ran down her dark cheeks and onto the jigsaw table runner. I sat in uncomfortable silence, watching with a heavy heart as she palmed away her tears. She took a shuddering sigh.

"A few days later, my uncle came home from work unusually early. He asked my aunt to take us children outside and shut the door behind us. I knew something was wrong by the haggard expression on his face. It'll stay with me as long as I live. When the door was closed, we stayed by it, our ears pressed against the wood as we listened.

"I'll never forget my aunt's cries. They were bloodcurdling. It was like someone was stabbing her heart over and over. Terrified, we all ran back inside. My uncle was in a chair, pale and sweating. My aunt was on the floor, sobbing and hugging herself like a frightened child.

"Yasmin, my oldest cousin, asked what had happened. My aunt sat up, her eyes bloodshot from tears, and said to me the words that would shatter my life: *your parents are dead.*"

I found that I was crying, too. How awful, for your mum and dad to be gone like that, with no warning. I sniffled, reaching to take my mum's hand. She gripped me with warm fingers.

"I don't remember much of that day. It's all a haze. People came in and out of my aunt's house; ladies patted me on the head like I was a small animal that didn't know what was going on. Weeks went by in a blur. Sometimes at night I could pretend that Mother and Father were still alive, that they were safe at home and it was all a just nightmare. I later found out that our house had been hit by a bomb. 'They died instantly,' someone told me. 'We couldn't bring them to your uncle's house because their bodies were blown apart'."

"Oh God," I whispered, sniffling. This was awful to hear, but still I listened.

"We had to bury what was left of them straight away. Even now, I feel like part of me disappeared along with them. I missed my parents so much and I was angry at everyone and everything around me.

I became bitter and resentful, and my heart filled with hate.

"After about half a year, my aunt screamed that she couldn't handle my emotional outbursts any longer. I don't blame her for that now. She had so much on her plate already, and how are you supposed to deal with an angry 11-year-old who blames the world and herself for her parents' deaths? Every day I said that I wished I'd died with them.

"I got shipped from one relative to another, moving every couple of months when the women of the house couldn't handle me. 'Worse than an animal,' one said. 'Like trying to care for five boys at once,' said another. They didn't let me work outside and made me an in-house maid for the wives and children. I'd clean from dawn until dusk every day, as payment for staying and eating their food. My uncles weren't poor, but they had just enough for their families. Even though I worked, I always felt like a burden to them. As the days went by, I lost myself more and more. I was in a never-ending cycle of work, sleep, eat. My heart was broken, and I felt more alone than ever.

"When I was 17, Uncle Amara, a distant cousin of my mother's, decided it was time to marry me off. It didn't make much difference to me – clean for a family or clean for a husband, it was the same. It wasn't as if I had a choice in the matter anyway. Their daughters were always asked if they wanted to marry, and if they said, 'I'm not ready yet, Papa,' it wasn't a problem. They had their mothers to fight for them. No such luck for me."

I thought about what my reaction would be if my father suddenly demanded I marry, without giving me a choice. I couldn't imagine how my mother must have felt.

"Without ceremony, I was married off to the baker's son, Sammy. He was 30 years old – a quiet man that worked with his father. I hoped he'd be kind and treat me well, and to my relief, he did. But he never loved me, and I didn't love him.

"After two years, we had a baby girl."

This made me sit up. I hadn't known I had an older sister. When my mother looked at me, her eyes were full of sadness.

"We named her Amal, after my mother. She was my life, my heart, and my soul. I understood now what motherhood meant. It was unconditional love, and I remembered my mother and everything she had done for me, all the sacrifices she made, all her hopes and ambitions. I understood how heartbroken she was when I couldn't be a doctor, how much it must have hurt when I was sent away. Though Sammy couldn't understand, I cried like I'd never cried before. It was as if my parents had passed away just that night. All the grief and anger came out of me. I could finally breathe again.

"Six months after Amal was born, she developed a high fever. A terrible rash appeared all over her body and her temperature wouldn't go down. I tried everything – a cool bath, lemon and honey mixed with water – but nothing would work. There weren't any doctors or hospitals open; everywhere was either shut up or full due to the constant clashes between us and the Israelis. I didn't sleep for two days as I kept watch over her, listening to her poor little cries. By the third, I knew if we didn't get her help, she'd die.

"I woke Sammy up in the middle of the night and told him he had to find a doctor. 'I don't care if it isn't safe,' I remember screaming at him. 'Go to the end of the earth if you have to. If you don't go, I will.' He argued, but finally left. Amal kept getting worse, her throat tore from crying and her skin burned at my touch. I felt so powerless, all I could do was sing and rock her to try to make her feel better.

"It was worse when she stopped crying."

I was clutching the table with white knuckles, desperate not to hear anymore yet unable to do anything but listen. I was watching my mother travel through the painful memories I didn't know she had.

"She went silent and grew cold. I didn't know what to do. I grabbed her and banged on my neighbour Zahra's door, yelling for her to open up. It felt like a century before she finally did. I just handed her Amal, unable to find my voice. She let me in and rubbed Amal's chest and feet. I prayed to every god I knew. I wept, I bargained, I begged – everything. But it didn't matter. Zahra looked up at me and said the words that shattered my world, 'I'm sorry, Nada, she's gone.'

"I couldn't do anything but stare at her. 'Gone where?' I managed to say. I was in denial, of course. I knew what she meant. I knew why my daughter was lying there, not moving, her poor little eyes open and not seeing me. Zahra didn't reply. I snatched Amal up, cradling her, begging her to come back, trying to warm her because her body was so cold. Her fingers – I remember – her tiny fingers were so blue."

She spoke easily now, the words slipping out of

her, as though she'd opened the dam – the waters crashed through. A single tear ran down her cheek as she looked at the wall past me, lost in memories.

"I refused to believe that she'd died. My daughter was not dead. Zahra cried until the sun came up while I sat there, clutching Amal. I hated myself for it, but not one tear came. It was as if they'd all dried up. Sammy found a doctor and came home, and when he saw we weren't there, he knew something was wrong. He saw the lights on in Zahra's home, so he knocked on her door and she let them both in.

"The doctor took Amal from my arms and looked her over. It was barely a minute before he said to me, 'I'm sorry. She's gone.' I didn't blink, I didn't move. It still hadn't sunk in. Sammy buckled beside me and wrapped his arms around my waist, sobbing. By midday, they'd buried her tiny body. I asked Sammy to have her buried next to my parents.

"For the next six months, I spent every minute of my time at the graveyard, sitting near her. I wasn't living anymore; I hadn't lived since I was 11 and my parents were still alive. What hope Amal had given me had now been brutally snatched from me too. I wanted to fade away. I'd lost everything.

What meagre relationship I'd had with Sammy diminished – we were always fighting. One day, we had a big argument and he slapped me. I knew in that moment I wasn't going to waste one more second of my life with him.

"That night, I went to my uncle's house to tell him it was over between Sammy and I and that I wanted a divorce. 'If you divorce Sammy, your family will disown you,' my uncle said. 'No one will let you stay here again. You know that, don't you? Thousands of people have lost their children in this war and are functioning normally. Why can't you do the same? At least she died of natural causes, and wasn't shot or blown up.'

"His cold words cut me deeper than his refusal to let me divorce. 'Sammy is a good man,' he continued. 'He might have a temper, but life is hard for everyone right now. He's given you shelter and food; you shouldn't be so ungrateful.' I just stared at him, lost for words. In that moment, I hated my whole family. If I went ahead with the divorce, I was on my own, but I didn't care. I'd been alone most of my life. I got up and left without saying another word to him.

"I divorced Sammy and found a job across the country as a seamstress. The owner was an old

Christian lady named Maria who felt sorry for me and let me sleep in her house, which was also a workshop."

I badly wanted to interrupt and ask, "Isn't it hypocritical that you stayed in a Christian's house when you won't even let me look at anyone of a different religion?" But if I did that, I'd get a clip around the ear and sent to bed. And I desperately wanted to hear the rest of this story.

"I had no friends or family. My uncle was true to his word; they all disowned me and pretended I didn't exist. They said I'd brought shame to the family." She gave a scoff, wiping away a fresh tear. "The years passed, and I got used to my fairly peaceful life in the workshop. I still thought about Amal every day, of course, but with each passing month, the pain lessened, little by little. As for Maria, she became my best friend. She treated me like the daughter she'd always wanted. She told me that many years ago, she'd been married herself. When her mother-in-law found out that she couldn't have children, she made her son divorce her."

"How awful," I couldn't help saying. Mum nodded.

"Maria never remarried. She said she felt incomplete. She had no idea how much I could relate to her words.

"I don't know why, but I didn't tell her about Amal. Speaking her name out loud would have opened fresh wounds.

"Though our religions weren't the same, I was surprised at the similarities. Maria would go with me when I felt like praying at the mosque, and I went to church with her on Sundays. Though I never opened my heart up to her Jesus, I learnt a lot about Christianity.

"One day, I went out to get Maria's medication from a nearby pharmacy. As I was walking, I tripped over a loose rock and grazed the palms of my hands. A young man came over and asked me if I was okay. I said thank you, I was fine, and walked it off. A week later, I was opening the windows and saw a man sitting on a milk crate opposite the workshop. I didn't take much notice of him and minded my own business. Every morning after that, when I opened the window, I found him sitting on the milk crate, watching me. When I closed the window that night, he threw something through it. It was a stone, and to it was tied a small piece of paper."

I sat up, listening.

"*My name is Salim*, the letter said. *I don't know if you remember me, but I saw you near the pharmacy a few weeks ago. You're very beautiful. I followed you that day to see where you live. The moment I saw you, I knew you were the one."*

I let out a nervous laugh, imagining my father sending Mum a letter like some lovesick fool. "He followed you home?" I chuckled. "Stalker, much?"

"I didn't know how to feel about it at the time." Mum smiled. "I remember thinking it must be a mistake. I wasn't sure what to do, so I showed the letter to Maria. She said, 'I think the boy likes you.' I remember looking up at her warm brown eyes and saying, 'I'm not lovable'."

Pity surged in me for my mother. Abandoned, neglected, and disowned. She'd really believed she wasn't worthy of love. I took her hand again, and her fingers didn't slip from my grip.

"'Who would love a broken woman?' I asked. 'A divorced woman? He doesn't know a thing about me. I'm not marriage material, Maria.'

"'Look at me, child,' Maria said to me. 'Don't make the same mistakes I did. You'll grow old and find no one next to you, like me. You're still young and have the world at your feet. Give your heart a chance; you never know where it might lead you. At least talk to him. Where's the harm in that?'

"That night, I couldn't sleep. I thought about

the letter and what Maria had said. If I gave Salim a chance, could I be a wife and mother again? Could I find happiness?"

I already knew the answers to these questions, of course, but I was enjoying this part of the story. Mum had gotten the happy ending she deserved.

"As you might be able to guess, I decided to follow Maria's advice." Mum smiled. "I gave him a chance. The next morning, I scribbled a note to him. *My name is Nada. If you really want to get to know me, you must come to the workshop and speak to me in front of Maria, the owner.* That morning, I opened the window and, as always, found him sitting waiting for me. I threw the letter to him and waited until he'd read it. He smiled at me and nodded his head."

Mum's eyes were dreamy as she smiled to herself. I wondered what my father looked like back then, whether she'd fancied him at first glance.

"He came to the workshop and knocked on the door. Maria opened it and let him inside. I remember she had this little smile on her face as she offered him tea. 'Well, Nada, don't be shy,' she said. I sat on the couch opposite him, but I was suddenly too embarrassed to say anything or even look at him. Maria, I saw in the corner of my eye, watched him like a hawk. 'Now, Salim, was it?

Nada has told me you're interested in getting to know her. Is this correct?'

"'Yes, ma'am. I am.'

"'I'm a traditional lady,' said Maria. I could tell she was rather enjoying herself. 'If you have intentions of knowing this young woman, to marry her, then you're welcome to come to my workshop to talk to her, but only when I'm here. If you're not serious and you just want to pass some time, I'm sorry, but I cannot allow it.'

"Your dad almost fell off his chair! 'No, ma'am, I'm serious! I am!' he said.

"'Very well, then, son. Tell us a little about yourself.'

"It felt like a job interview. Salim looked shocked, too, as though she was interrogating him. 'I'm 25 years old,' he said finally. 'I live with my mother in a little house not far from here. I have two older brothers, they're both married. We own a little land and have a plot of olive trees.'

"I watched Salim while he was talking. He had blue eyes like the sky, and I thought he was very handsome. I hardly noticed when Maria spoke to me. 'Come, child, tell Salim a little about yourself.' She sounded excited. I cleared my throat, unsure what to say. At first I just gawped at them both like a clueless schoolgirl."

It was hard to imagine my mother so shy.

"'Come on now, Nada, we don't have all day,' said Maria. So, I said, 'I'm 25 years old, too. I've been married before and had one child who… who passed away.' It took a lot for me to say that. Maria glanced up at me, her kind eyes filled with pity. She did not speak, and instead bowed her head for me to keep going. I took a deep breath to calm the pain swelling in my chest. 'My parents died when I was young, and my remaining family disowned me for divorcing my husband. I won't blame you if you're not interested anymore.' By the time I'd finished, I was whispering. I'll never forget your father's response: 'It changes nothing,' he said. 'I'm not interested in the past'."

My heart swelled with love and admiration for my dad. "He loved you so much he didn't care about the past," I said, grinning. Mum nodded.

"That made me smile. For the first time in a long time, I felt some sort of hope. I hadn't realised until that moment how in despair I'd been, how I'd been traipsing in mud in the dark, not really living.

"Of course, words alone weren't enough for Maria. She laid down some rules for him. 'You may come three times a week to the workshop,' she said, 'and talk to Nada for two hours. At all times,

I must be present.' Maybe she could tell that this might lead to something more and was being the protective mother she'd always wanted to be. Salim agreed to her conditions and left. For the next couple of weeks, we got to know each other. Soon, I was looking forward to his visits. I discovered what a kind, caring man he was, not only from what he said, but how he behaved – how he really listened to me when I spoke. I was falling for this man and knew he was my soulmate. After a year, we decided to get married. Maria asked him to bring his family to ask for my hand in marriage.

"'Nada, my dear, don't you want to ask your uncles to come?' 'No,' I said firmly. They'd ignored me for years, so why reach out now? 'I have no family. Except you.'

"That night, Salim came to Maria's workshop with his family. I was so nervous." Mum gave a laugh. "I was scared his mother wouldn't like me or we wouldn't get along. Salim's visits had been a new light in my life. It was going so well I was sure something would show up to spoil it.

"Maria explained my story to them. We had to do the marriage papers in court as I had no family to act as witnesses. They agreed, and his mother hugged me. She said she hoped I'd see her as a mother figure instead of a mother-in-law."

I thought about my grandmother, imagining a younger version of her welcoming my damaged, broken mother so graciously into her home.

"We got married the next week. I moved in with them and never looked back."

CHAPTER 3

I didn't know what to say, so I stood and hugged her. I heard her sniffle, which made me cry, too. To think Mum had been through all of that.

"Why didn't you tell me any of this before?" I asked, wiping at my tears.

"You were too young," she sighed, pulling away. Her dark eyes pooled, though she was smiling. "Honestly, I never really planned to tell you at all, for what benefit would it give? I only told you this so you don't befriend Hannah."

My hands slid from hers and I sank onto the

chair. Of course, now we were getting to the point.

"The Israelis played a part in my parents' deaths, in Amal's death. They bombed my home and because of them, there was no doctor around to save my daughter. Nisma, my darling, with the situation in our country now, we don't have the luxury of being tolerant or philosophical or giving people the benefit of the doubt. You might see this as mean or cruel, but it's the truth." She reached out and tucked a stray strand of my hair behind my ear. "As you can see, the Zionists and the Palestinians are in constant war with each other. Hannah might seem like a nice girl, but she still has a father, a grandfather, cousins, uncles, who might be playing a part in our peoples' suffering. I don't trust any of them, and neither should you, Nisma."

I listened to my mother and nodded. I might not agree, but at least now I understood. I felt sorry for her.

"Let's eat," I said finally, glancing at the covered food. "I'll call Grandma and the boys."

That night, I tossed and turned, thinking about what my mother had told me. Whenever I closed my eyes, flashes of her sobbing while she cradled a lifeless baby girl, or being told that she was being disowned, or meeting my dad for the first time, flooded my vision. Compassion and discomfort muddled my mind.

I felt guilty that I'd never paid much attention to her, always focusing on what I wanted. I'd always thought it was because she was uneducated that she was close-minded. But she had more life experience than anyone I knew. I'd been wrong. If she wrote a book about her life, it could be a bestseller.

Finally, close to midnight, I started to doze off, but a sudden noise jolted me back awake.

I rushed to the window and my heart turned cold. Hannah's father was outside, staggering as he dragged his wife by the hair down the street. Her screams sent goosebumps up and down my arms.

To my horror, he punched her hard in the face and her body went limp. He yanked her again. She spat blood, leaving a thin trail of red as he pulled her along the road. Tears sprung in my eyes at the violence. *He's killing her!*

Hannah ran out of the house, pushing her father, screaming. Even without understanding Hebrew, I knew what she was saying: *leave her alone!*

I didn't think. I threw on a dressing gown and ran downstairs, not heeding the noise I was making. I ran outside onto the pavement, swallowing as I saw Hannah's mum lying on the ground. Her father was gone.

"Please help me, Nisma!" Hannah cried in English. Tears were streaming down her face. "My mother's going to die!"

I didn't need asking twice.

We crouched down and lifted her mother by the arms. She was unconscious, her head lolling side to side. Blood spurted from her nose and down a cut near her eyebrow.

"My father stole her bracelet," Hannah sniffled. "He needs it for... for..." her eyebrows knitted together. "I don't know the English word. He tries to win money, but he loses it."

"Gambling?" I said, recalling the word from an English dictionary I'd been studying. Hannah nodded, whispering something in Hebrew to her mother as we put her arms around our necks, lugging her over to my place.

We couldn't take her home. If Hannah's dad came back, he'd hurt her again.

We helped her mum up the stairs and through

my front door. It was hard work. By the time we finally got her onto the couch, we were panting, dripping with sweat. Hannah's face was full of worry as she looked at her mum. She was stirring, her eyes flickering, still bleeding from her head. Hannah sniffled, wiping at the blood on her mother's lip with her sleeve.

"Wait here. I'll get my mum and dad."

I went to their bedroom, wondering if our noise had woken them up. In that moment, I didn't care if they'd be angry about what I'd done. I couldn't leave Hannah and her mum on the street like that, ignoring their pain just because they were different to us. It wasn't right.

"Mum, Dad. Get up, quick," I said, flying into their room and switching on the light. Mum jolted up, her hair in a mess. Dad was slower, squinting as he sat up.

"What's wrong, Nisma? Are your brothers okay?" Mum asked, scrambling out of bed in her nightgown.

"They're fine," I blurted out quickly. "Look… Hannah and her mum are here."

"Hannah who?" Dad said, groggy. He yawned as he swung his feet out of bed.

"Our neighbour, Dad!" I said. "She's losing

blood! Quick, we have to help her!"

That woke him up. My parents followed me as I ran to the living room. Mum's face paled when she saw Hannah's mum, bleeding onto the carpet. She looked even worse in the light – bright red blood on her face and bruised where she'd hit her head – her body limp and weak. Hannah quietly cried beside her.

"She needs a doctor," said Dad. "She's losing blood. Nisma, get some cloths from the kitchen and place them on her head until I come back."

"Come back from where, Salim?" asked my mum, her eyes wide.

"I'm going to look for a doctor," Dad pulled on a jacket.

"At this time? It's not safe."

"Have a heart, Nada. She'll die if I don't find someone to help us."

I was glad Hannah couldn't understand what they were saying.

"Well, you heard your father," said Mum briskly. I quickly did as she asked, getting the softest and thickest cloths we had and holding them against Hannah's mum's head. She winced as I did, and the cloth rapidly turned crimson. I used five of them, the floor soon covered in bloody rags.

"The boys still asleep?" I asked Mum as she helped, wiping blood from Hannah's mum's nose and prodding to check for more injuries. She groaned when we touched her ribs.

Dad wasn't gone long, but to us, it felt like an eternity. Finally, he arrived with a doctor – a pale, tired-looking man carrying a briefcase. We all scrambled out of the way as the doctor pulled up a stool, his mouth a straight, serious line as he examined her.

"Hey," I said softly in English to Hannah as she sat hugging herself. "It's okay. The doctor's here now."

I didn't really believe the words I was saying, but I had to make her feel better somehow. I glanced over at my mother, expecting to find her glaring at me for talking to Hannah, but she was watching the doctor work, worry on her face. I wondered if she was thinking about the doctor who had examined little Amal. The thought made worry crawl in my guts like angry snakes.

The sun had started to rise when the doctor finally leaned back and said to my parents, "She's lucky to be alive."

I quickly translated as the doctor put her on a drip to keep her hydrated. He bandaged her head and made her more comfortable on the couch.

"She needs a hospital, really, but in our current situation, this is the best we can do for now," he said. "The next 24 hours are crucial. No food or drink. If she starts to vomit, a hospital is what she'll need."

I translated as best as I could, and Hannah immediately replied, "I'll stay with her. I'll check her for vomiting and everything."

"I'll give her an injection so she can sleep," the doctor said, administering something that made Hannah's mum relax. Her body lost tension and her breathing became slower.

My father thanked and paid the doctor as he showed him the way out. I could hear movement from my brothers' bedroom. My grandmother appeared, staring at the woman she didn't recognise on our sofa.

"What's wrong?" she asked us, looking around before her eyes landed on Hannah. She withered under her gaze. "Who are these people, Nada?"

I let my mum fill her in as I took Hannah's hand. Her lip was trembling, a tear sliding down her cheek. I silently prayed that my mother would not cause a scene and instead find it in her heart to show compassion to these poor people.

"It's okay," I said softly, putting my arms around her and pulling her in for a hug. "She'll be okay.

Your mum's strong, you know."

"Thank you so much, Nisma," she whispered back. "For helping us."

"Don't be silly, you'd have done the same for us."

Hannah avoided my eye line.

Dad appeared, looking tired. "Nisma, tell me everything that happened."

Hannah trembled beside me as I recounted the details. "I woke up earlier to screaming and shouting," I said. "Hannah's father, he was—" I glanced over at Hannah's mum, "he was hurting her. Badly. He stole her bracelet and threw them out of the house. I couldn't leave them."

"What kind of person could do that?" asked Dad in disbelief, sinking onto the stool the doctor had sat on. "Nisma, please ask Hannah why her father hit her mother."

I translated, struggling through my high school English and wishing I had a dictionary at hand. Hannah nodded frantically as she understood.

"My dad wanted her to give him her bracelet," she sniffled. "She said no, because it was from my grandmother. She gave it to her before she died. He wanted to sell it to pay off his…" her eyebrows knitted. "To give money back to someone else."

I nodded, knowing the Arabic word for 'debt',

but not the English one. I encouraged her to go on.

"She said no, so he got angry. When he drinks, he gets angry easily." Another tear fell, dripping onto her clasped hands in her lap.

I translated, and my father shook his head. "Some people don't deserve to have families. Nisma, ask Hannah if she has any family she can turn to."

When I asked in English, she shook her head, her dark curls waving side to side. "We don't have any relatives on my mother's side here. They all live in America. My father's family disowned us because of his gambling and drinking."

"What's your mother's name?" I asked.

"Lilly," she said, her voice soft.

It was strange interpreting between Hannah and my parents, but it was vital. Aside from some difficult words, we managed to communicate between the four of us.

"Hannah, my dear, you and your mother are welcome to stay here as long as you need to. If you want anything, let Nisma know and I'll try to get it. Nisma?" he asked me, "Get my jacket, please. There's no point going back to sleep now."

Lilly was asleep on the couch, her chest rising and falling while the IV drip pumped hydration into her veins. Hannah stroked her hand, exhausted.

"I'll go to the mosque and then head off to work," he said. "Nisma, get some pillows and sleep in the lounge room with Hannah and Lilly. I'd like you to keep an eye on them."

Asmar and Fadi were silent, watching Lilly with large eyes. It was rare to see them so quiet. My grandmother pottered around the kitchen, staying out of the way, perhaps. I wondered how she felt about this.

I heard Mother whispering furiously to Dad as he headed for the front door. I'm not sure why she bothered speaking so quietly, it's not like Hannah or her mum could understand anyway.

"Salim, you're not serious about letting these people stay here?" she hissed like an angry snake. "You want us to help the enemy? If the neighbours find out we're hosting a Jewish family, we'll never hear the end of it."

"To hell with the neighbours," said Dad calmly. "What's happened to you, Nada? Since when have you been so heartless? Didn't Maria take you in even though she was Christian and you were not?"

Mum said nothing. I listened, holding my breath. It was rare for my mother to be silenced by my dad.

"A real Muslim loves all of his neighbours and is to be kind to them regardless of whether they are kin, a stranger, or, in this case, a Jewish Israeli. I would hope that if the roles were reversed, they would help you and Nisma. I love you Nada, but I must put my foot down: while our guests are here, I don't want to hear 'enemy' this, or 'those people' that. Do you understand?"

I peeked around the hallway corner to see my mother silently nodding. Mum often won arguments with Dad, but she could see there wasn't any point pursuing this one. As she closed the door behind him, I caught her mumbling, "That man has lost his mind. He wants to feed the Zionists meat."

I backed into the living room, pretending I didn't hear her. I was exhausted. It was already dawn, but we could still get some rest. I grabbed the blanket and pillows from my room and we settled in the lounge to sleep, though Hannah didn't close her eyes much at all. Alert, she sat and watched her mother intently, regularly checking her temperature and breathing. I understood. If my mum was hurt, I wouldn't be able to rest either.

"Let me take over. Get some sleep," I said finally, and took shift of caring for Lilly. The doctor had said that if she got sick, we needed to take her to a hospital. I couldn't imagine that would be possible, so I hoped and prayed she'd stay asleep. Hannah finally got a few hours of rest, her nose blocked from crying. She looked much younger, somehow, curled up on the floor.

I woke her at around eight o'clock, so tired I couldn't stay awake any longer. I felt bad for waking her, but I hadn't had much sleep myself. I collapsed on my bed and fell asleep as soon as I hit the mattress. At around midday, I woke up to the sounds of activity in the house.

"Good morning," I said as I approached the kitchen. My grandmother and Hannah were at the table, peeling potatoes.

"Good afternoon, you mean," Grandma chuckled. "Wash your hands and come help us, please."

I settled between them, picking up a potato and a peeler and acting as translator.

"How is your mother today, Hannah?" my grandma asked.

"She's okay, I think," Hannah said. Her eyes were red rimmed from tears, but she spoke with a steady voice. I was glad we'd both concentrated in English class. "She's been in and out of sleep. I think the injection the doctor gave her is strong because she's still pretty out of it."

"Where are Mum and the boys?" I asked.

"Their shoes are ripped to shreds." Grandma clicked her tongue, depositing potato skins in a bag. "She took them to a repairer."

"Your grandmother's so sweet, Nisma," Hannah said. "We can't understand each other's words, but we managed to get to potato peeling by pointing and making noises."

It was the first time I'd seen her smile in ages. I grinned back.

After we finished chopping the vegetables, I gave Hannah some fresh clothes. They were a little big on her, but that couldn't be helped. As I took Lilly's temperature, Mum and the boys returned. She was shouting at them.

"Never, ever take children with you to the market," she groaned. "They drive me insane."

Asmar and Fadi giggled together. "We made Mum look for us." Mum looked like she was about to reach her boiling point.

"It's not funny," I snapped at them. "You shouldn't make her worry. Cheeky monkeys."

They ran off to their room to colour. Hannah waved in greeting to my mother, who bristled at her and stalked off.

Crestfallen, Hannah sat beside me. "Your mother hates me, doesn't she."

"She doesn't hate you," I said, avoiding her eyes. "She'll come round, don't worry. Want to watch TV?"

I desperately wanted to distract her, to keep her mind from worrying about her mother, or mine for that matter.

"Yeah, okay," she said, her voice quiet. "My father sold our TV last year."

I felt cold as I looked at her. "For gambling?" I whispered.

She nodded, looking into her lap.

"Why doesn't your mum leave him, Hannah?" I asked. "Why does she put up with all his beatings?"

"It's not that easy," she said. "She has no one to turn to. My family on her side are all in America and they want nothing to do with us. They're rich and educated and were against my mother's marriage from the beginning. When Mum was 18, Dad was her family's accountant. They owned a grocery store downtown and Mum met Dad when she went to help out in the shop. He was charming and polite back then, she said."

I thought about my own mother's story of how she met my father in a shop. Except they were still happy. The ending hadn't been the same for Lilly.

"When her mother – my grandmother – passed away two years later, her father decided to move the family to America. But my mum refused to go with them, saying she wanted to marry my dad. My grandfather was furious that his only daughter was going to marry 'the help'. He didn't approve of the wedding at all. He went to the shop that day and got my uncles to beat up my father because they thought he'd touched my mother. Maybe he did, I don't know."

She sniffled, wiping her nose on her sleeve.

"They hit my father so hard they broke his hip. When my mother found out what they'd done, she was furious. She made up her mind that she was going to marry my father whether her family approved or not. Well, they got married, and my grandfather and uncles moved to America that year without saying goodbye to Mum."

My heart clenched as I thought about all the times I'd disobeyed my parents. Lilly's dad had just been trying to do what was best for her, but she hadn't been able to see it.

"My mother always said that the first year of their marriage was good. Father treated her well and worked hard. They tried to make amends with

Mum's family a few times, but it never panned out. As my father lost hope that his in-laws would forgive them, he started to change.

"He told her it was her fault that they didn't have money. 'You're from a rich family,' he complained. 'They should be helping us.' Mum thought that after they had me, things would settle down, but he only got worse."

I wanted to hug Hannah. Tears were pouring down her cheeks now. Instead, I handed her a tissue, which she blew noisily before carrying on.

"He told her he never loved her, and he'd only married her for her family's wealth. When I was five, he started gambling and beating her up. In the beginning, he only did it sometimes, and she always forgave him. He always cried and said he was sorry, kissing all her bruises, swearing he would never drink or be stupid with money again. And she believed him. She always forgave him." She sighed and looked over towards the living room where Lilly was still sleeping. I watched in silence. Hannah's mum had been sleeping for nearly 12 hours already.

"It was worse when he owed people money. He always found a way to blame her – he would snap at the slightest thing. I'd drop some food on the floor, and he'd lose his temper. Mum would burn dinner, and he'd start punching her. Mum was always crying, and I was always scared."

I couldn't imagine living in a household like that. Grandmother got grumpy sometimes, and my mum was a little crazy when she was angry with me or the twins, but I could never imagine her or Dad hitting us.

"It got worse and worse. He beat her up nearly every day. My mum is too ashamed to leave. She'd rather die than have her family say, 'I told you so,' or worse, pity her."

Hannah's voice cracked at the last word, and I hugged her, both of us crying. I didn't have any words for her.

Despite our differences, we were so much the same. We cried the same tears, went to school, loved our families. We were all humans; that's what it came down to.

"I don't feel like watching TV anymore, Nisma."

"Neither do I," I said. "Let's check on your mum."

The living room light was off, but daylight streamed through the window. Lilly's hair was in a tangle; the bruising on her cheek and around her eyes had turned a bright, purplish-yellow – her skin pale. As we approached, her eyes flickered open.

She looked at Hannah, then at me, then back to her daughter. Her lips parted but nothing came out except a weak croak.

Hannah knelt beside her mother and stroked her hair, speaking softly to her as I hovered by the doorway, sadness filling me. For a moment, it looked like Hannah was the mother and Lilly the child.

Lilly nodded slowly, her eyelids drooping until she was sleeping again. I backed out of the room and busied myself with helping Grandma set the table for dinner. My brothers were already there, chattering in their foreign twin tongue while my grandmother sat between them.

I told my mother what Hannah had said about Lilly. Mum shook her head.

"Some men need to be burnt alive," she snarled, making me raise my eyebrows. "It's a disgusting thing, beating up a woman. But it doesn't change the fact that Hannah and Lilly are Zionists, Nisma."

"Please don't start with that again," I groaned.

She pursed her lips, setting down the cutlery with a little more force than was necessary. Just as she began pouring the meaty, sweet-smelling soup into bowls, Dad walked through the door.

"You're on time, Daddy," I beamed as Asmar and

Fadi wriggled out of their seats to jump all over him.

"Daddy!" they shrieked, running circles around him. "Daddy, Daddy!"

"Okay, now, boys," I laughed. "Let him breathe."

Dad scooped them both up, planting kisses on each of their cheeks before setting them down at the table. "Mmm, something smells delicious."

I watched him, trying to picture him getting mad and hitting my mother. Try as I might, I just couldn't imagine it happening. I was so lucky to have such a gentle father. I'd taken that for granted until yesterday.

My brothers clambered onto Dad's lap as soon as he sat down, even though they hadn't finished their dinner yet. Fadi had sauce all over his chin, making my mother click her tongue in annoyance.

"How are our guests, Nada?" he asked her, grabbing a cloth to wipe Fadi's face.

"They're fine," said Mum shortly. "We're treating them like royalty." Her words dripped with sarcasm. When Mum wasn't looking, Dad rolled his eyes at her. I felt a rush of mirth and covered my mouth to stifle a giggle. Maybe Dad was as tired of her attitude about Hannah and Lilly as I was.

"Well, I brought home two pieces of shanks," he

said. "I'd like you to make it into a soup for Lilly. The poor woman needs nutrients to build up her strength. The doctor said no food or drink for a day, so she'll be starving after that." He held up a bag and my mother placed it in the fridge, not answering him.

"Call Hannah, please, Nisma, to sit and have dinner with us."

I went to fetch her, and Hannah came and sat shyly next me. Dad greeted her with a warm smile, giving her a bowl of soup and a thick piece of bread.

"Thank you," she said in English. Dad understood that, at least, and gave her an encouraging nod.

"And how are you, *Yamma*?" he asked, getting up and kissing my grandmother's hand. My grandma made several small comments about her day while Mum served the rest of the soup, leaving us to eat in silence. Even the boys were quiet, munching on bread as they stared at Hannah with wide eyes.

The awkwardness was suffocating, like the room had been drained of oxygen. Mum cleared her throat once or twice, saying nothing. Grandma slurped quietly. Finally, it was Dad who broke the silence. "So, Nisma, how's your day been?"

"Um, fine," I said. Normally I could make up something on the spot, but I was drawing a blank.

"And how about school, Hannah? What's your favourite class?"

I quickly translated, and Hannah jumped, her cheeks pinking.

"Hannah's an A-grade student, Dad," I said. "She wants to become a doctor."

Mum scoffed. I ignored her.

"Well, that's excellent to hear, dear," said Dad cheerfully. Anyone who didn't know him well would think he was truly upbeat, but I could tell he was pretending for Hannah's sake. "Education is your only weapon in this world. I wanted to be a doctor too, but unfortunately it wasn't on the cards for me."

I translated as best I could, sadness filling me. Dad would have made a wonderful doctor. Of course, it was a great job to have in general, but especially now when doctors were so in demand.

"There is a university in Tel Aviv, sir," said Hannah. "Nisma could go there."

When I repeated her words in Arabic, Mum nearly choked on her soup.

"Hannah, you are an ignorant girl indeed," she snapped.

Hannah may not have known the words, but she understood the tone. She lowered her gaze.

"Mum said… um, that's impossible," I said quietly.

"Well, we will see," said Dad. "But if Nisma's to go to university, it'll be abroad, not here. If I could pay for her to go."

"Dad," I said, torn between exasperation and gratitude. "Where would we ever get that kind of money? We barely have enough for food."

"You never know, Nisma," Dad winked. "If your grades are good, you might get a scholarship."

"I hope so, Daddy."

He was talking nonsense to keep the conversation going, but the thought of going to university somewhere in Europe or America was incredibly exciting to me. I imagined being away from the bombs and danger, walking down a high street in London or shopping in New York. I indulged myself in this happy little daydream for a moment until Mum picked up the bowls and put the kettle over the fire. The tension loosened in Hannah's shoulders a little as we sat in the lounge room drinking spiced tea.

Lilly was still on the sofa, and Hannah and I helped prop her up onto some pillows. There was more colour in her cheeks and she was responding to questions. After Hannah helped her mother use the bathroom, she came back and sat on the couch, her face contorting in pain. Pity filled me.

Lilly mumbled something to her daughter in Hebrew.

"Can my mother have some water?" Hannah asked me.

"Water is okay, but nothing else until tomorrow," said Mum, reappearing a moment later with a mug. Lilly sipped quietly. Her dark hair was a tangled mess and the cut on her head was starting to scab.

Dad finished his tea, then sat on a stool near Lilly, scooting close to her. "I want you to know you're both safe here," he said as I translated. "You and your daughter are my guests, and if either of you need anything, you let me know at once."

It was a double translation; I translated into English for Hannah, and Hannah translated to Hebrew to tell her mother. I hoped the meaning came across the same way even if the words were different.

Lilly looked at my dad, her eyes pooling. A tear slid down her face. She said something in such a pitiful tone that it broke my heart even before Hannah translated.

"Why are you helping my daughter and I?"

My father's eyebrows shot up in surprise at the question. "What do you mean, why? You're our neighbour. You were hurt. Did you expect us to leave you on the street to die? I'm sure if we'd needed help, you'd have done the same."

My mother gave a harsh laugh at his words. Dad shot her a glare and she rose to her feet, mumbling about putting the twins to bed.

Hannah looked uncomfortable as she translated her mother's next words. "If it was you or your family, Salim, I know in my heart I wouldn't have helped you. That's the truth. I was always taught that your ancestors stole our land and we were fighting for what is rightly ours. We always believed that," Hannah took a breath, her glance falling to the floor, "…the more of you that died, the better it was."

Hannah's trembling words made me feel cold. So Lilly and my mother weren't so different, after all.

Dad looked up at me expectantly and I reluctantly translated for him. His muscles tensed when I told him what she'd said. I wondered if he was angry.

"Well, let's not dwell on the past or what other people have done," he said finally, his voice even. "We don't always have to believe what our parents have told us. God gave us our own brains to think with and make conclusions about matters. I'll let you rest," he added, getting to his feet. "It's getting late."

Lilly nodded as Dad avoided her eyes. I was torn between exasperation and respect for her honesty. I had a sudden, terrible image of myself and my mother bleeding to death on the street, a healthy Lilly at her doorway, closing the door on us.

Well, that won't happen, because my father isn't an abusive drunk. It was a wicked thought, but I couldn't help it. I was tired of both her and my mother's intolerance. Maybe if more people learned to forgive, there wouldn't be so much fighting.

I watched from the doorway as Hannah tucked her mother in and kissed her forehead.

"I'm sorry," she whispered to me afterwards.

"No need," I said back. "We aren't responsible for what our parents think."

I left them in the lounge and retreated to my room, my head spinning. I took out my diary and wrote on an empty page.

Who's to blame for all the hatred in the world?

In a bold, red pen, I answered: *Parents. Ignorance. Misunderstanding!*

I closed the diary with a snap and put it in my top drawer, carefully tucking it under several notebooks. When I turned off the light and slipped into bed, I fell asleep at once.

CHAPTER 4

When I woke the next morning, I felt unrested, like I'd only slept a few minutes. I dragged myself out of bed, stifling a yawn, and headed for the kitchen. Mum and Grandma were drinking tea at the table. The boys had already left for school.

"I didn't want to disturb your beauty sleep, Your Highness," said Mum mockingly. "It's past 11, Nisma. You're already behind on your chores. You're supposed to be grounded, you know, not on holiday."

"Okay, Mum," I said, irritated that I was being

scolded just as I'd woken up. If it was nearly noon, why was I so tired?

I washed my face and tied my hair in a plait before joining them for a quick lunch. "Are Hannah and Lilly awake?" I asked between mouthfuls. "Are they all right?"

"Don't talk with your mouth full, Nisma," Mum snapped. "They're still asleep. Your father brought the doctor in at around six this morning to remove the drip from the Zionist. God knows how much we're out of pocket because of that."

I ignored the jibe, sipping water. The IV drip was out; that had to be a good sign.

Mum said to my grandmother, "Why wouldn't you sleep until lunchtime if you had servants at your beck and call? I wouldn't want to get out of bed at all, would you?"

My grandma, white-haired and serene as always, gave a smiling nod. I sighed as loudly as I dared, getting up to clean my plate. Sometimes it seemed my mum and grandma shared the same brain. They agreed on everything. I always thought that mothers and daughters-in-law were not supposed to get along, at least sometimes. But my mum and grandmother were like 'peas in a pod', as my dad would say.

I left them agreeing with each other and went to check on Hannah and Lilly. I raised my hand to knock on the lounge door when it suddenly opened. Hannah looked refreshed, the worry almost completely drained from her face. She wore the same robe I'd lent her the day before.

"Good morning," she said, smiling.

"Hi," I greeted back. "How's your mum doing today?"

"She's much better. She got up early and took a bath and drank a big glass of water. The doctor came this morning to take the drip from her arm and said she could eat and drink normally now."

"That's great," I said, making up my mind to cook Lilly a big lunch as soon as I could.

"The doctor said she's past the most dangerous stage," said Hannah. "But she still needs lots of rest. Your parents won't mind if she stays a little longer, will they?"

An awkward silence fell between us. "It's fine," I said finally. "Would you both like some breakfast?"

"I'm not hungry," she said, waving her hand. "I'll make Mum something when she wakes up."

I had to finish my chores, so I reassured Hannah she could call for me if she needed anything.

"Would you like any help?" she offered. "You'll

be done quicker."

I hesitated. Like Mum had said, I was supposed to be grounded. She might blow her top if she saw Hannah doing half my work for me.

"You can peel vegetables for dinner later, if you like," I said. "I hate doing that."

It didn't occur to me until I was scrubbing the floor that afternoon that Hannah was probably bored out of her mind. She hadn't brought anything from her house, and she couldn't even read any of our books. We did not dare return to their house to pick up any items. Her dad's location was unknown, and he could be back anytime. Hannah truly believed that the next time he saw them, he would kill them.

A few hours before dinner, we found the kitchen empty, and I gave Hannah a bag of potatoes and a knife. She'd only peeled two when sudden noise erupted from outside. It sounded like shouting.

I opened the window and peered out. From the kitchen, we had a good view of the street below. Hannah gasped as she joined my side. There was her father, swaying and yelling at the top of his voice, in what I could barely detect as very broken Arabic. When he switched to Hebrew, Hannah translated in a shaky, tear-filled voice.

"My whore wife is staying with those filthy Arabs," he screamed. Several passers-by had stopped to listen, gawking at him and our house. "She has fallen in love with the Arab! She has betrayed Judaism and she's betrayed Israel!"

He threw a bottle to the ground in his rage. His cheeks were a blushed dark red – his clothes unkempt, like he'd been sleeping in them. Fear gripped me as I swallowed hard, shutting the window. He knew Hannah and Lilly were here.

Startled by the noise, my mother and grandmother joined me in peering through the closed glass. In the lounge, Lilly was awake, her lips tight as she listened to her husband roaring below. Hannah ran to her mother, wrapping her arms around her as they both began to cry.

"We'll be a disgrace," moaned Mum, holding her head. "The neighbourhood will never stop talking about this. Oh, the shame. What will we tell everyone?"

I turned away in disgust. Lilly and Hannah were terrified for their lives and my mother was still worried about her reputation. I pretended not to hear her as my grandmother nodded along to her rant. I was getting tired of them both.

"Don't listen to him," I said to Hannah, forcing

a smile. "You're safe here with us."

"We can't stay here," said Hannah, her eyes glassy with tears. "My father won't leave us alone. He knows where we are. Nisma, my mother and I have been talking. She wants to go to America to be with her family."

"I thought they disowned her?" I said bluntly.

Hannah nodded. "Yes, but if she asks her father for forgiveness, it might work. It's our only hope."

We could still hear her father raging outside. America sounded like a good gamble to me.

"We talked about it before. We could go to the American consulate in Tel Aviv and try and get visas. Mum still has her earrings, but I've heard the flights are expensive." She sighed.

"I wish I could help," I said. "But I have nothing to give you." My words made me blush. I didn't have a single *agora* to my name, and even if we had money, Mum wouldn't spare anything for them. She'd almost passed out giving them soup and tea.

Hannah wrapped her arms around me, pulling me into a tight hug. I inhaled her flowery smell, hugging her back.

"You've already done so much for us, Nisma," she said. "If I ever had a sister, she wouldn't have treated me as well as you have."

Her mother hugged me next, and Hannah translated her whispered words, "You have a big heart, Nisma. You're a good girl."

My heart bled for them both.

Hannah's dad got tired of screaming at our house and finally sloped off, leaving an eerie silence in his wake. We tried to lighten the mood by playing with Asmar and Fadi, but there was still a heaviness, an invisible fear we couldn't shake off. What if he tried to get into our house? What if he brought more men with him? There was nothing much we'd be able to do to fight him off.

I waited impatiently for my father. He finally came home after dinnertime and sat in silence as I updated him on what had happened. He said nothing, his lips pressed in a thin line.

"Well, Dad?" I said when he didn't answer me. "What are we going to do?"

"He doesn't scare me," said my father, stroking his greying beard. "He's a dog; let him bark. If he was a real man, he wouldn't hurt his own family."

"How are we going to get the money together to fly Hannah and Lilly to America?"

He made an impatient noise. "We barely have enough for this house and the food in our bellies, Nisma," he said. Seeing my crestfallen expression, he sighed and reached over to pet my head, something he hadn't done since I was a child. "I'll see what I can do tomorrow."

I was glad my father wasn't heartless like my mum. I might have known her childhood story and everything she had been through, but I still didn't believe it was an excuse to carry that much hate and anger. The truth of the matter was that we were ruled by corruption on both sides. In all my heart, I believed the government fuelled the hatred of the people – a divided country is much easier to rule than a united one.

"I'm off to bed," said my dad finally, rubbing his face. "Goodnight, sweetheart."

"'Night, Daddy," I whispered.

That night, I couldn't sleep. I listened to the far-off sounds of barking dogs and shouting voices, scared we'd suddenly hear Hannah's father yelling or banging on our door. I felt safer with Dad here, but tomorrow he'd be out at work again.

I finally took out my diary. I hadn't written much since this had all happened, just my angsty letters about parents and ignorance and misunderstanding. I picked up my pen and scribbled, my anxiety battling exhaustion.

Parents bring children into this world and pass on their hates, likes, fears, hopes and dreams. They don't leave the child a blank slate or clean canvas, the way Allah created them. They fill him up with ignorance from their own upbringing.

Sometimes people are misunderstood — their actions are taken differently to their intentions. In the end, hatred is born out of all these things and generations suffer the consequences.

I didn't know if my tired rambling made any sense, or whether I was right or wrong. I turned to a new page when the whole house suddenly shuddered, a shockwave rippling through my head and throwing me onto the mattress. I lay in shock, a piercing ringing in my ears as the windows shook violently, threatening to shatter. Outside, a dog gave a panicked bark as screams echoed up and down the neighbourhood.

Asmar and Fadi cried from their room as I sat up, reeling from the sound. Where had the bomb landed? It sounded close. My mother's soothing coos filtered up the hall as she consoled my brothers.

As much as the noise had stunned me, I didn't bother looking outside to check the aftermath. Living in Qu'laif forced you to get used to these things. Every now and then, groups of teenage boys would throw handmade bombs into the streets, usually resulting in a brief gun fight and Israeli police chasing them into the darkness. If it was up to me, anyone caught doing such an act would be hanged in the town square, regardless of religion or political stance. Sometimes these small bombs landed in people's houses and killed them. Even worse, the next morning the culprits would sit around celebrating and congratulating each other as if they had made some great contribution to humanity. It stirred a lot of anger in me.

Sighing – my heartbeat finally slowing to normal – I chose a bright pink pen and drew love hearts around the page. Then I wrote in bullet points all my dreams, numbering them from one to ten. The higher it was on the list, the more badly I wanted it.

1. *To have my own money so I can buy whatever I want to eat.*

2. *To be able to afford nice clothes.*

3. *To own two pairs of good shoes, one for school and one for special occasions.*

4. *To buy toys for the twins.*

5.   *To buy Mum and Grandma new clothes and a bottle of perfume each.*

6.   *To get Daddy some proper work boots instead of the flip flops he always wears.*

7.   *To graduate from school.*

8.   *To be able to go to university.*

9.   *To get a good job.*

10.   *To live in peace and not worry that if one of us leaves the house, we might not come back.*

Tears splashed onto the page as I finished writing. These weren't dreams. They were basic human rights. Why was it so hard for us to live like the rest of the world? I closed my diary with a snap and tucked it into the drawer, settling down to try and sleep.

Scenes of Hannah's father and bombs haunted my dreams, and I woke with a thin layer of sweat coating my sheets. Faint light gently filtered through the windows as the rest of the house remained still. It had to be early in the morning. Typical – the one day I didn't have chores, and I was up at the crack of dawn.

Outside, men were talking on the street. I listened to their dull voices, hoping to catch a snippet of conversation about last night's bomb. I recognised one of them; it was our neighbour, Amin.

Amin sold Turkish coffee off a cart outside his house, and people liked to go there to relax and chat. The stories I heard from my bedroom never ceased to amaze me. At around five or six in the morning, men would head to Amin's after praying at the mosque, where they would sip coffee and debate whatever was on their minds. Everything from politics to religion – even their sex lives – was up for discussion. No topic was off limits to them.

Their voices would rise as the conversations grew fiery, which was often. In fact, the only thing they seemed to be able to agree on was that America was the root of *all* their problems, even if they were simply complaining about toilet paper.

This morning was no different. A scraping of chairs muddled with Amin's voice echoed up the street. "I will not tolerate you mocking each other's religions!" he thundered. "Go take your barbarism somewhere else!"

Tony and Ahmad, I reckoned. A Christian and a Muslim, they were always bumping heads and bickering over religion. They both worked at the bakery down the street and got along just fine until someone brought up the topic of faith. If only they were tolerant of one another's beliefs, they could have been best friends. They turned into different people when they argued, and were sort of famous in our town because their quarrelling could get so heated.

"Stop yelling, Amin," said Tony. "We'll change the topic."

"No, I'm not in the mood to put up with you today," Amin replied, shortly. "Pay and leave. You can come back tomorrow if you behave."

The men grumbled as their coins clinked along the counter. Then, the place was silent. Nobody argued with Amin when he was angry.

I closed the curtains, rolling my eyes at their foolishness. I swear, writers from Hollywood should come live on our street to get ideas for their movies. It was always action-packed.

As much as Tony and Ahmad argued over religion, them both being Arab meant they could at least get along well enough to have some sort of relationship. The Palestinians and Israelis had no such luck. My musings quickly turned to thoughts of Hannah and her mother. Had the bomb frightened them, too?

When I knew I wouldn't get back to sleep, I washed and found my parents in the kitchen, eating breakfast together.

"Good morning," I said as brightly as I could.

"Good morning, Nisma," said Dad, planting a whiskery kiss on my cheek.

"You're up early," Mum remarked, and she actually smiled.

"There's a first time for everything. Could I please have some tea?"

She seemed to be in a better mood this morning. The strong scent of sage and mint wafted through the kitchen, filling my nostrils. I fetched a mug from the cupboard.

"I kept having nightmares last night," I told her when she asked why I was awake. "And Tony and Ahmad were fighting again, so I couldn't get back to sleep."

"What was today's topic?" Dad laughed. "Politics?"

"Religion," I said through a mouthful of curried eggs.

"I bet Ahmad and Tony were stars of the show," Mum said, clicking her tongue in annoyance. "Those people have no manners. Your brothers are always being woken up with their noise."

We glossed over the bomb that had gone off in the night. It was such a normal occurrence, that we saw little point dwelling on it. Finally, I asked, "Mum, where are Hannah and Lilly? Are they still asleep?"

"No," she said, her voice cold. "They already left for the American embassy to apply for visas. I hope they get them, so they'll leave us alone." She took an angry sip of tea. "I can't even face going down to the market right now. I feel like everyone's whispering about us behind our backs."

"Oh, stop it, Nada," my dad snapped. "How many times have I told you that they're our guests?"

An argument was brewing. When Dad spoke back to her, it generally blew up, much like last night's bomb. I quickly interjected, "Daddy, can I go to work with you today?"

His eyebrows shot up in surprise. "You've never asked to go with me before."

"I know," I said, "but it's harvest time. I'd like to see how you pick the olives. I'm tired of staying at home today, and—" I looked at Mum, who was glaring down at her tea as though it had insulted her. "And today is the last day of me being grounded, right?"

"Nisma, you're a girl," Mum sighed. "What

would you find interesting in the olive fields?"

"Please, *Yamma*," I begged. "I'm so bored here. I have no chores today."

"Let her come, Nada," said Dad. "She'll keep me company. Get dressed, then, quickly. I'm leaving soon."

I fled the room before Mum could change his mind. As I headed out, I heard her snap, "You just can't say no to her, can you, Salim? You're spoiling her."

CHAPTER 5

It was still early morning – cool and fresh – the early October wind blowing on my cheeks. It ruffled Dad's beard, making me giggle. I couldn't remember the last time we'd been alone together like this.

When we reached the valley, many of the other farmers were there already, picking olives from the trees, or hitting them with branches and catching those that fell into the mesh on the ground. A few raised their hands in greeting as my dad and I passed. Along the other side of the field were

Israelis dressed in green army gear and carrying rifles, faces stern as they watched over the fields.

Seeing them shout and fight made me nervous. I hoped they wouldn't have to use their guns. "Why are they arguing, Daddy?"

Dad's face was tense. "The soldiers won't let the Arab farmers take their harvest out of the valley without paying a fee. They say it's for protection."

"Protection from what?"

"Thieves," he sneered. "Some people pay it to avoid the headache. Others argue and say they wouldn't pay it even if it killed them. It's the soldiers who are stealing the crops in the first place."

I swallowed. The farmers here were mostly poor. They needed all the profits they could get, just like us.

"Do you pay them, Daddy?"

"When I was young, I didn't," he said, taking out a roll of mesh from his backpack. "Sometimes I was beaten up for it, and a few times they burned my harvest to teach me a lesson."

Tears sprung up in my eyes. It was all so unfair. I imagined a younger version of my father watching his olive trees burn to the ground, black smoke belching into the sky.

"Since we had you, I've always paid," he said

darkly. "I can't afford to be gallant, and often resisting isn't worth it. Some people see me as a coward, especially those folks over there." He pointed towards a nearby group of farmers. Most of them were young; the older ones shook their heads as they gathered olives. "But I don't care. What's the point of gallantry if it's going to cost me my crops and my family?"

I wanted to hug him. Giving the Israeli soldiers a wide berth, we headed for our section of the land – a small patch with only about 50 trees. There were no fences between our plot and the neighbour's, with each huddle of trees bleeding into the next. The farmers' efforts knew no borders, and they often pooled their labour to assist one another with their crops. When the end of harvest season came around, they all chipped in to prepare the land for the following year.

Our trees had been in the family for generations. Dad's dad had passed them onto him, and his dad had owned them before that. Undoubtedly, Asmar and Fadi would inherit the plot one day too, and the tradition would continue for as long as the Shahin name carried on. The olive trees were in our blood.

Dad's older brothers, Amir and Yusef, had tried to pressure him into selling the plot after my grandfather had died. "Sell it to the Israelis, Salim!" Amir had said. "If you don't, you will always be a poor man!"

But my father was resolute, vowing to never part with even one tree.

"You are a fool, Salim," said Yusef, his words laced with contempt. "I pity your family. They will spend their days with hungry bellies because of your stubbornness. You will never be able to support them off the back of those paltry trees."

As we approached the first row of trees, we were met by two farmers, slapping at the branches. Fat, ripe olives flew past their heads like rain.

"Good morning, gentlemen," Dad greeted.

"Morning, sir," they both replied, their gazes lingering on me for a moment before returning to their work.

"What can I do to help, Daddy?"

"See that?" Dad pointed to the mesh wiring on the ground. "I'd like you to pick the olives from it and put them into those crates." Several wooden boxes lay along the ground. "Can you do that?"

"Sure can!" I was excited. The breeze felt good and there was an earthy scent of soil and nature that filtered through the air. Green meadows filled with ripe fruit stretched for miles.

Mum had packed us boiled potatoes and eggs with salad for lunch. Eating outside after sweating from a morning of hard work somehow made the food taste even better. We worked all afternoon too, and I must have collected hundreds of olives before seven o'clock came and the sun began to set. As we packed up our things, three soldiers approached us. Dad stood a little in front of me, his body tensing.

"How are things, Salim?" said the nearest, a bearded man with intense hazel eyes beneath an army hat. "Looks like you're having a good season this year."

"I was before you three rocked up," said Dad. "The eye is a powerful weapon." There was bitterness in his voice, a sort of defeated tone that I didn't like. These men had hurt him before.

"What, you believe in that bullshit?" remarked another soldier. He had a patch of streaked blond on his chin that made him look like a goat.

"What do you want?" Dad sighed. "I'm in no mood to have a debate with you. You'll get your fee like always."

"Who's the pretty young lady, Salim?" said Hazel-Eyes, tilting his head to look at me as I cowered behind my father like a child. My heart started to thump. The other workers continued packing like nothing was going on. The men held their rifles like trophies, a proud display of their power.

My father pushed me further behind him. His hands were trembling, sending a wave of terror through me. "That's none of your business."

The three of them laughed – harsh, mocking sounds. "Why the animosity, Salim? You know we just want to be friends," said Goatee.

"Who'd want to be friends with you?" Dad snarled. He grabbed my hand, snapping at his workers, "Do you have all those crates packed?"

"Yes, sir," the nearest squeaked.

Dad grabbed his bag and we set off home. The soldiers didn't follow us.

"Filthy scumbags," Dad snarled. He was still clutching my hand. His palm was sweaty. "They have no respect for anyone."

"It's okay, Dad," I said. "Don't get angry. Please. They were probably just bored or something." My insides felt like ice, scared that a fight would erupt and the soldiers would take him.

"Those three are troublemakers, Nisma," Dad said, his steps so hard and fast that I had to jog to keep up. "I hadn't seen them for a while. They were all moved to different posts because of the fights they were having with the farmers. God help us now that they're stationed here again," he groaned, rubbing his eyes. "Not one day will pass without trouble. Nisma—" he suddenly stopped, looking at me with intensity. "Please don't mention any of this to your mother. You know what she's like."

"I know, Dad," I said. "I won't say anything, I promise."

When we got home, Hannah and Lilly had returned from the embassy, looking tired and a little worse for wear. They were in the lounge, quietly talking while Grandma and Mum prepared dinner, the rich scent of frying eggplant wafting through the house.

Asmar and Fadi were playing some rough game on the floor, wrestling and punching each other. As Dad stepped into the house behind me, the boys jumped to their feet and ran to him, yelling, "Daddy! Nisma!" like they hadn't seen us in a year. Fadi wrapped his pudgy little arms around my waist and I couldn't help smiling. It felt nice to be needed.

"Set the table, please, Nada, while I wash and pray," Dad called to the kitchen after he'd finished making a fuss of my little brothers.

"Okay, *albi*," Mum shouted back.

I grabbed my brothers around the waists, and they giggled and squirmed as I carried them back to the lounge room.

"Hi, Hannah, how was your day? Did you get the visas?"

I sat on the floor before them as Asmar and Fadi ran off to play. I wondered if Mum had offered them any water to wash with; they both looked tired and were wearing the same clothes as yesterday. I made a mental note to grab some extra things for Hannah and see if Mum could find it in her heart to give up an old dress or something for Lilly.

"Our day was okay," said Hannah. "A lot of paperwork. My hand's killing me from all the writing. It was in English and some of it was hard. I had to get the staff to help me a few times. I think they got annoyed with me."

"Oh," I said, my heart sinking. "I guess those English lessons have paid off, right?"

We shared a guilty giggle. "Well, we applied to the Australian and British consulate, too. Whichever one offers us a visa first, we'll take it."

"But you don't have family in those countries," I pointed out. "It'll be hard for you both."

I immediately scolded myself for being so negative. Hannah and Lilly needed support now, not misery. *I'm turning into my mother.*

"Mum tried to call my grandpa in America," said Hannah, taking her mother's hand. Lilly was lying back on the couch, her eyes closed. "But… um… when he heard her voice, he said, 'I have no daughter' and hung up. So it looks like wherever we go, we're on our own."

Cold shock filled me. Even after all these years, Hannah's grandpa was still angry?

"What about the plane tickets?" I asked, swallowing my suddenly parched throat.

"We tried to go to some Jewish charities, but they said they didn't help people that want to abandon Israel." Her voice shook now, brown eyes glassy. "We did sell Mum's earrings, but we still need about 800 American dollars just for the flights. Maybe we can find someone to lend us the money."

"Let's have dinner," I said as brightly as I could, getting to my feet. "I'll talk to my dad and see if he knows anyone who might be able to help."

After dinner, we drank spiced tea in the lounge. When Mum took the cups to the kitchen, Dad perched on a stool near Lilly and took three US$100 notes out of his wallet. Lilly gasped, looking down at the money with wide eyes.

"Nisma, tell Hannah to take this. It's all I managed to borrow."

It was then I realised Dad hadn't gone for a wash at all, but had slipped out to do what he could for our Jewish neighbours.

Lilly took the money with shaking fingers and burst into tears. Hannah hugged her while I beamed at them both.

"This is a great start! You only need another $500 now," I said, hoping my bright tone got through to Lilly. "Hopefully we'll be able to get that together soon. I'm going to bed; I have school in the morning."

They bid us goodnight and I gave them some fresh clothes before heading to my room, suddenly exhausted. I set my alarm for 6:30 am, wondering how long it would take to get back into my regular sleep pattern. My body ached after gathering all those olives; it was no wonder my father fell asleep quickly every night.

CHAPTER 6

I stretched, feeling refreshed as the early morning sunlight streamed through the gap in my curtains. I was excited to go back to school and escape the daily housework. Being grounded had lasted *forever*.

I quickly dressed and went to wake up Fadi and Asmar. Asmar was already awake, playing with a toy under his sheets. Fadi looked dead to the world.

I helped them dress into their uniforms, thankful that they were behaving themselves.

"Hurry guys, or we'll be late," I whispered,

ushering them to the kitchen. The house seemed unusually quiet this morning. I knocked gently on the lounge door and found that Hannah and Lilly were already up and dressed.

"We're going to see if there are some other charities that'll help us," Hannah explained when I asked why they were already awake. It looked like Hannah wouldn't be coming to school today.

"Good luck. See you when I get home," I whispered before heading back to the kitchen to pack lunch for myself and the boys. As we were on our way out, Mum rushed from the bedroom, her hair tousled.

"It's okay, Mum. I already packed their lunches and dressed them. We're leaving now."

Mum groaned, sagging against a beam as she held her head. "Nisma, you're a lifesaver," she said, gathering me into a rare hug. She kissed my cheek, then the boys'. "It's so unlike me to sleep in."

Feeling warm and fuzzy from Mum's affection, I dropped the boys off at their school and made my way towards my own, stepping carefully along the cracked cement and uneven ground. As I approached the main school building, I counted the boarded-up windows that peppered the wall closest to me. Seven. One more than the last time I was here. I doubted they'd ever get around to fixing them. As I walked through the gates, a group of nearby kids suddenly stopped talking, staring at me.

"What?" I asked, uneasy. Perhaps there was a bug on me.

Whispers and stares followed me as I headed for the building. "Guys, look who's back! The Jew sympathiser!" I whipped around to see a boy from my class jeering at me.

My neck burned. Heat spread across my cheeks. So, everyone knew. Somehow, word had spread about Hannah and her mother staying at our place. I held my head high, ignoring him. It wasn't anyone's business.

The gossip followed me all morning, and by first class, was becoming unbearable. As I made my way toward a seat at the back of the room, meandering through the congested maze of teenage bodies, nearby students scooted their desks away as though they'd catch something. I sat down, avoiding their gaze.

A blackboard stood at the head of the class, its corners cracked. Many of the chairs were falling apart, planted wearily along the grimy stone floors. An old, inked message marked the corner of my desk. I ran my fingers over the splintered wood.

The first class was history – of all the classes! Mr Yacoub was going to rip me to shreds, I was sure of it. I sat low in my seat, wishing I could turn invisible. If I'd known coming back would be like this, I wouldn't have come.

"Good morning, students," said Mr Yacoub, his voice shrill.

"Good morning, Mr Yacoub," we mumbled. His dark eyes darted like a hawk's around the classroom until they fell on me. My heart sank.

"My, my," he remarked, his face lighting up. "Look who's decided to finally turn up for class."

I felt like a cornered mouse being taunted by a cat. Several students tittered as my cheeks burned.

"Miss Nisma, would you care to tell your fellow classmates why you've been absent from school for so long?"

The titters turned to giggles and jeers. I stared at my desk, nerves bubbling in my guts. I wished the ground would open up and swallow me whole.

"Personal reasons, sir," I finally mumbled. It wasn't fair. My mother had kept me off school; it wasn't my fault.

"Personal reasons, you say," he came over, his hands behind his back as he looked down at me. "There are rumours going around that you and your father are protecting a couple of Jewish whores."

The class exploded into laughter as if Mr Yacoub had told the joke of the century. Anger replaced shame, burning in my chest. It was none of his business. I didn't look up to meet his eyes – I wouldn't give him the pleasure of breaking me.

"Quiet," he finally snapped at the class, as though he wasn't the one causing the disturbance in the first place. The lesson finally began.

His eyes locked onto mine as he said, "Right then, class. Today's topic is 'how traitors and sympathisers support terrorism and bring a country down'."

Someone snickered behind me. I felt like screaming. Addressing the whole class, Mr Yacoub said, "As you're all aware, terrorism is a huge problem in our world. The biggest terror organisations are in the United States of America and other Western countries like them. How do these countries become so violent? Well, I can tell you, they always had help from traitors of the countries they attack."

My fists clenched beneath my desk. Nobody was laughing now.

"If every Palestinian was to open their house to the Jews, Palestine would never be free from occupation. Isn't that right, Nisma?"

His final needle of words flipped a switch in my brain. I couldn't hold back my anger any longer. "No!" I yelled. "That's not right at all."

Several people gasped, but I didn't care. "It's none of your business what my family and I do in our own home or who we sympathise with." I was breathing fire, nostrils flaring as I stood glaring at my teacher. My chair was toppled over, thrown to the floor. I couldn't even remember getting to my feet. "America and Israel aren't the only terrorists in the world. The Arab countries can be far worse. They allow terrorism to happen by turning a blind eye. People here can't have a decent life because people like you are degrading them and turning them into puppets!"

Mr Yacoub's jaw clenched, his eyes wide. I waited for his bellows, for him to call me stupid and throw me out of the room. But, his words did not come. Perhaps I had shocked him into silence. My tirade continued, unremitting.

"If The West truly created terrorism, then we were manufacturers of that creation. Just the other night, a bomb went off near my house. I never hear of kids in America afraid that their parents may never come home, or scared they'll wake up with their neighbourhood blown apart!"

My teacher composed himself, standing straight. He was several inches taller than me. "What filth you spout," he snarled. "It's people like you and your father who need to be tried for treason."

Now he was insulting my father. I couldn't take it anymore. I snatched up my bag from the floor, shoving my notebook and pencil inside. I could feel everyone's eyes on me. "It's people like *you* who can't bear the truth. You blame everyone but yourselves. People like you allow terrorism to happen. Our people were once leaders of innovation, but you reduced us to nothing."

I was almost screaming now, my voice ringing through the room and bouncing off the walls — little bombs of venom raining on pretentious, deaf ears. Already, I was in trouble, but once I started, I couldn't stop.

"Our generation only knows how to clap for corrupt politicians that are puppets of The West. Kids like me, like *us*, can't get a real education anymore because they're too busy fleeing bombs and grenades, or scraping for their next meal, or looking after orphaned family members." An image of my mother flashed before my eyes, living with her aunt and working instead of learning and playing. "And you still tell me America and Israel are the problem? Just like a pig who rolls in his own shit then complains of a bad smell, that is exactly what you, and people that support your absurd ideologies, are!"

The class was so silent you'd hear a drop of water splash on the floor. They stared between me and Mr Yacoub. His chest rose and fell, fire in his eyes as he glared down at me. But I didn't feel scared; I was consumed with blind hatred. Then he finally found his voice.

"Get out of my classroom, you filthy traitor!" he bellowed.

I let out a shrieking laugh. I don't know where I got my confidence from, but all I could feel was disdain. "Don't you worry, *Sir*. I was just leaving."

I closed the door behind me, and a wave of dread washed over me at once. I'd barely been back at school five minutes, and this time I'd be lucky not to be expelled. Mum was going to go off the rails.

But a part of me didn't care. I wasn't going to keep my mouth shut any longer. Part of why bad things continue to happen is that people are too scared to stand up. No longer. I'd stand up for what was right, even if it cost me my education... or my life.

I refused to be like everyone else, hiding behind a fake narrative and ideology. A life full of hate and fear isn't a life, it's a death sentence. The streets were quiet as I walked home, my steps hard and fast. Fury battled through me, the memory of Mr Yacoub's twisted face clear in my mind like strobe lightning.

As I got closer to home, though, my steps faltered. The adrenaline was starting to wear off. But I wasn't going to be a puppet – like my mother burying her head in the sand, or my father being forced to pay a tithe to the Israeli soldiers on his olive tree land.

I knocked softly on the door to our house. It felt strange being back so early, before even lunchtime. My grandmother called something from inside and the door opened with a cautious creak, springing wide only after she saw me. Her white hair was a messy tangle and she was still wearing her robe.

"Nisma, child, what's wrong?" she asked, almost dragging me in and looking me up and down. "Did something happen? Are your brothers all right?"

"All fine, Grandma," I said. "Let's go inside and I'll tell you."

I dumped my schoolbag on the sofa, wondering for the first time what had happened at school after I'd left. No doubt Mr Yacoub would have been a firecracker for the rest of the class. I didn't care. My classmates had mocked me for letting Hannah and Lilly stay. I wondered how many of them silently agreed with me. I imagined all of us rising against our teachers and school, our voices combining to something meaningful that everyone would hear. I scoffed. *Not in a million years.*

"Where's Mum?" I asked as I put the kettle on.

"She went to the market to buy vegetables," said Grandma, settling herself on one of the dining chairs and looking at me with concerned blue eyes. "Now tell me what brings you back from school so early."

I made us tea and we sat together. There was no avoiding it; she was worried. I quickly told her everything that had happened, sparing no detail. She didn't say a word the whole time. Her eyes, so like my father's, looked between mine. Though she said nothing, I felt like she was scanning me. I took a sip of tea as she pressed her lips together.

"Do you really want to hear what I have to say, or would you prefer me to tell you what you'd like to hear?" she asked.

The question surprised me. Often, especially with my mother or my teachers, I would try to say what was expected of me, not what I truly thought. My grandma had likely been through the same thing.

"I'd like to know what you think, Grandma."

"You overreacted, Nisma," she said. "Yes, Mr Yacoub did cross some boundaries, but you took it a step further."

I swallowed. My grandmother usually nodded and agreed with everyone, tranquil in her own world. It was rare to hear her telling me off. Shame flushed in me. "Of all my grandchildren, Nisma, you are the most challenging." She sighed, leaning back. Her eyes looked tired. Then she did something I did not expect; she chuckled.

"You're just like your father when he was your age," she smiled, shaking her head. "But life has tamed him. My child, you need to understand that war brings out the worst in people far more than it brings out the best. You're still young, Nisma, and you don't understand. Many people will simply never forgive the invasion of our country. Even if all the Jews packed up and left tomorrow morning, they would always hate them."

Steam rose from the teacups between us. Outside was quiet; everyone was working.

"But Grandma, the problem isn't only the Jews. It's a lot of things," I said. "Why do we blame them for everything? There have been more atrocities in this country in the last 50 years than the rest of the world has seen in centuries."

"It's not that simple," she sighed, before taking a long sip of tea. "Although your intentions might be clean and come from a kind heart, you need to bite your tongue, especially before your teachers. No doubt Mr Yacoub didn't appreciate a teenage girl shouting back at him."

I gave a slow nod. Already, I was regretting my words to my teacher.

"You can't blurt out everything you think or feel, especially when it comes to religion or politics. You'll get yourself – all of us – into trouble."

"Mr Yacoub said Dad and I are traitors for letting Hannah and Lilly stay here," I said as I clutched at my skirt, anger rippling through me at the memory.

"Well, you know that your mother and I were against them staying here, but you and your father insisted. We knew this would happen. People like to jump to conclusions and make assumptions; they're not interested in the full story, especially when it comes to the Israelis."

"That's for sure," I muttered.

"A convenient lie is easier than an inconvenient truth," said my grandma, reaching to pet my hand. "They don't want to hear or believe that any good could come from a Zionist's mouth. This is what your mother and I were afraid of. Who will want to ask for the hand of a traitor's daughter?" She gave another tired sigh, leaning back in her seat.

Worry filled me. I hadn't thought about the long-term repercussions of helping Hannah and Lilly. I thought that the rumours would stop soon, and things would calm down.

"My father isn't a traitor."

"I know he isn't," she said sincerely. "But other people don't."

"Well, to hell with what people think," I snapped, getting to my feet. "Maybe I don't want to get married anyway."

As the last words left my lips, the front door opened. There was the rustle of cloth and my mother walked in, her arms full with bags of groceries from the market.

"Nisma. I thought I heard you shouting," she

said in surprise. "What are you doing back from school so early?"

"She wasn't feeling well," said my grandma at once, getting to her feet beside me before I could respond. "She threw up, so they sent her home."

"Oh dear," said Mum. "You do look a little pale, dear. I hope you haven't caught a bug."

Grandma gave my hand a warning squeeze before helping my mum unpack the vegetables.

"I think I'm okay, Mum," I said, complying with the lie. "I, um, must have eaten something that upset my stomach."

I was feeling queasy, but it had nothing to do with anything I'd eaten. How long would it be until the school decided to report what I'd said to my parents?

"I'll make you some soup," said Mum, her voice kind. "Go and rest. I'll pick up your brothers from school today."

Guilt plagued me for lying. Why had Grandma protected me? I supposed she was just delaying the inevitable. Even if by some miracle my teacher didn't tell my parents what was going on, 50 other kids had seen my outburst. The news would be travelling around the school like a forest fire by now. Crazy Nisma, the traitor Zionist-lover. I'd never hear the end of it.

Mum would cry, probably. She'd ground me for a century and scream at my dad, "*Salim, your daughter will never get married now! You spoilt her so much to the extreme that she is uncontrollable!*"

Why did everything turn against me? All I'd wanted to do was help two people in need. Wouldn't I want someone's help if I were in their shoes? Wouldn't anyone?

I'd tried to have a quiet life, I really had, but people forced me to talk. I couldn't sit quietly and keep my thoughts to myself like my grandma could. I collapsed onto my bed, suddenly exhausted. I must have fallen asleep, because I opened my eyes to the sound of my father's voice in the kitchen. Mum had left a bowl of soup by my bed, but it was already cold.

I staggered to the kitchen to find Mum and Dad, quietly talking.

"Oh, Nisma, you're awake, dear," said my dad, hugging me. "Your mother was just telling me that you came back from school not feeling well today. What a shame, too, you were really looking forward to going back."

"Yes, Daddy, I came back from school today," I said in a small voice. The guilt tumbled inside me like a thunderstorm. I couldn't get Grandma to lie for me, and anyway, they'd probably find out soon enough. It was better they hear it from me first.

"I didn't come home because I wasn't feeling well," I said. "It's because I left the classroom."

Behind my mum, I spotted Grandma, sitting on her sofa and knitting, slowly closing her eyes and shaking her head. I couldn't help it. *You might be able to keep your mouth shut about things, Grandma, but I can't. I'm sorry.*

Mum glanced at me and abandoned her knife on the bench. She pulled up a chair beside my father, her face serious. I hated how she was looking at me. Concerned, not angry… not yet.

"What do you mean, Nisma?" she asked gently. It was the calm before the storm.

I told them everything, my gaze sinking lower and lower until I was staring at my lap, not daring to meet my mother's eyes. I could sense the smoke coming out of her nostrils. Out of the corner of my eye, I saw my dad with his hands on his forehead, his eyes closed. There was a silence that stretched between us all, a black hole ready to swallow me up.

When Dad spoke, his voice was teary. "You know, Nisma, you're just like I was at your age," he said finally. Grandma had said the same thing.

"I always said what I thought, but that has now cost you, my daughter. I would hate it to cost you your life." He reached over to pull me into a one-armed hug, something I wasn't expecting. He gave a watery sigh and kissed my forehead. "I'm proud that you're my daughter. We've raised you well."

Emotion tumbled through me. My father was proud. I hugged him back, tears burning in my own eyes.

"Yes, bravo."

Mum's voice was cold, not like her own. I finally looked at her. Her brown eyes were narrowed, and she even gave a sarcastic clap. "What an honour it is, what an honour."

I swallowed, my throat tight. For the first time in my life, I felt truly scared of her. She leaned back, her arms crossed over her chest. "Like father, like daughter."

"Nada…"

"Instead of slapping her, you hug her, Salim! Say that you're proud!" Mum was on her feet now, her cheeks blushing an ugly red. "She left the classroom, shouted at her teacher, and made a mockery of our family, and you hug her? You *hug* her?"

She was screaming, spittle flying from her lips, throwing her hands up in violent gestures. I flinched.

She'd yelled before, many times, but never like this. She was trembling as she pointed at me.

"You'll be the reason I have a heart attack, Nisma. You and your father won't rest until I'm dead in my grave, will you? Why can't you be a normal child?" She was sobbing now, tears dribbling down her cheeks. I was crying, too. "Why can't you just go to school and come back without a problem? Why can't you keep your opinions to yourself? We'll be the talk of the town, mark my words. No one will ever ask for your hand in marriage. You'll grow old and die alone, and for what, Nisma? For ideas in your head? You can't change anything, none of us can. You want to change the world when we can barely afford to eat? How many times have I told you that ideas and opinions are a privilege for the rich and free, not the poor?" I wondered if her throat was going to tear. Her shrieks bounced off the walls. "In this country, it will cost you your life!"

She stopped for breath, her chest heaving up and down. Even Grandma had stopped knitting, her wrinkled face pale with worry. Mum held her head like she had a headache, letting out a heartbroken groan that sent goosebumps along my skin. I hated this. I hated how I'd hurt her.

"Nada," said my father. How was his voice so

calm? "What Nisma did was the right thing. Her teacher went overboard, singling her out like that. He didn't have the right to say any of those things or encourage the other children to jeer. To hell with school if our daughter's going to be bullied."

Mum made a noise between a scoff and a laugh, staring at her husband with her hands on her hips.

"I'll find a school that will accept her. And stop telling her she'll never get married. She might not want that anyway. She's a daddy's girl." Despite everything, he grinned at me.

"Fine. Fine!" Mum snapped. "Do as you and your daughter like, Salim. But I'm warning you, if anything happens to her, you'll never see me or the boys again."

Furious, she threw the tea towel in my dad's face and stormed out of the room. A door slammed somewhere in the house.

Dad sighed. "She'll come round, Nisma. Let her cool down and then we'll both talk to her."

I wasn't so sure, but hearing those words reassured me. Mum's fiery temper had us both on edge.

"I don't think Mum will be making dinner tonight, Dad," I said, trying to lighten the mood. We both chuckled. Grandma glanced sharply in our direction, silently scolding us for laughing when Mum was so upset.

"What should I have said to Nisma, Mum?" he asked, reaching over to take her hand and kiss her knuckles.

She snatched her fingers from his with a scowl. "Every word your wife said is the truth, and you know it, Salim. The only reason I didn't tell her what happened myself was so you could be here to control the situation."

"You don't think Nisma's teacher went overboard?"

"I do," said my grandmother softly. "But you know why, don't you, Salim? Your daughter is just like you were when you were young."

I felt a surge of pride. Yes, I was like my father. But Grandma was saying it like it worried her.

"Rebellious. Stubborn." Grandma's blue eyes found mine. "The only difference is that she's a girl, which makes it much worse."

Neither of us were laughing now.

"Girls aren't supposed to be like Nisma, saying these things and rebelling against their teachers. She's supposed to want shoes and clothes, to get married and be softly spoken. It is a dangerous thing for a young woman to be so opinionated, so outspoken. She should respect her tutors, her parents, and her ancestors. Mark my words, it will cost this family in the long run, more than you realise, my sweet boy."

Grandma leaned in, her face cold as stone, and a spike of fear ran through me. "Have you seen the state of Nada's health lately? She's always so tired and pale. You and your daughter torture that poor woman every day."

Those words hurt me. I never meant to hurt my mother. I couldn't always help what I said, or control the emotions I felt. Was I really affecting my mother's health? How would I forgive myself if I made her sick?

"We'll check Nada's health," said Dad, clocking the worry on my face. "Tomorrow I'll take her to the doctor, Mum, okay? She can get some blood work done and see if this really is affecting her health or not. I'm sure it isn't," he added, patting my shoulder and rolling his eyes. He shot Grandma a glare, a warning to stop scaring me. Then his expression softened. "I'll make it up to her, I promise. You know I don't try to upset her on purpose."

Grandma nodded, leaning back, her eyes sad as she looked at the door where my mother had left like a storm.

"I'll be making dinner tonight, ladies," proclaimed Dad with gusto. The tense atmosphere melted away as my grandma snorted with laughter.

"What will you be making, Salim? Some burnt eggs?"

I giggled, too. Dad had never been the best at cooking, not when my mother and grandma had always been around to take care of it.

"I should be insulted at that comment," said Dad, his back straightening, "But I'll prove you wrong."

I watched him grab an apron, tying it around his waist. "Watch and learn, missy."

There was a knock at the door, and I rushed to answer it. "Coming!"

It was Hannah and Lilly. I moved aside so they could come in. "Hi, Hannah."

They followed me into the kitchen where Dad was whistling, cutting up onions. Hannah and her mum burst into laughter at the sight of him, his apron clumsily tied. He turned to grin at them.

"I'm afraid Nada isn't feeling very well, so I'm cooking tonight."

I quickly translated, and they both nodded. We sat at the table and watched Dad struggle with peeling potatoes, which proved to be much more fun than sitting in the lounge. Grandma started knitting something for one of the twins, the radiantly calm expression had returned to her face like our conversation never happened.

"So, what have you been up to today, Hannah? Did you finalise your papers?"

"Not really," said Hannah with a sigh. "Dad's been causing trouble. He's put a no travel ban on my name at the airport and to lift it, we'll need a lot of money to bribe the officials. Money we don't have. I told Mum to forget about leaving and just find us a job each. I'm sure together we could afford a room or something. I'm sick of waiting all day at different departments and offices."

My heart filled with sympathy. They both looked shattered.

"They refuse to help us because our case isn't deemed urgent," Hannah continued. "And they keep asking why she wants to leave without my dad. They know we're staying here with you and they're not happy."

"They?" I asked, concern rippling through me. "Who's 'they'?"

"The government, Nisma," she said, meeting my eyes. "My dad must have tipped them off. They don't want Palestinians and Israelis to even be friends, let alone stay at each other's houses. They kept asking my mum, over and over, 'have you changed your religion? Are you in cahoots with these Arabs?' She said, 'No. Why do you want to know that?' Then the guy at the counter said, 'Well, we're aware that you're living with the enemy, so we have to check whether you've changed your religion'."

The whole thing was so ridiculous that I had no words for it and rolled my eyes instead. It wasn't any of the government's business where they were living, or who with. "Ignorant people," I finally muttered.

"After going to all those different places, Nisma, I'm starting to understand why our people hate each other so much," said Hannah. "It's the government that breeds all this hate and passes it onto their civilians. Many people don't know any better and simply believe everything they are told. Especially the people at those offices."

At least Hannah was on my side. I felt a little better telling her about what happened at school. She let out a gasp and her mum nudged her, asking what I was saying. As she translated, Lilly shook her head. Then she said in broken Arabic that left everyone in stunned silence, "God is big, Nisma. He sees and hears everything, my child."

She said the rest in Hebrew, and Hannah translated to English: "You're brave, Nisma. Much braver than us, and you have a good heart. But I agree with your mother."

I frowned. How could that be? After everything I'd told them and all they'd been through?

Lilly nodded, speaking rapid Hebrew. "Mum says if none of this had happened, she would never have changed her mind or views about your family, or about Palestinians." Hannah's cheeks blushed red. "She said if she was in your mother's shoes, she would have said and done a lot more than what your mother did." She smiled. "When we become mothers ourselves, we'll understand that everything they have done was always with the best of intentions, even if their children didn't see it that way." She gave me a private look that mirrored what I was thinking: *are you sure that's true?*

Hannah translated while her mother spoke, Lilly reaching across the table to take my hand. Her fingers were warm and thin. "You girls are the future, but you can't change everything alone. You must understand that, and really believe it. Otherwise, you could both get into serious trouble."

"I changed your views, though, didn't I?" I smiled at her.

Lilly nodded.

"Now it's your turn to change the ideas of one person," I said, giving her fingers a gentle squeeze to show I wasn't being argumentative. "Then they change someone else's, and that's how the world will evolve. We can't all sit back and expect the change to happen by itself; it must start somewhere."

We weren't living in this country; we were existing. Even with my father's arguably decent job olive farming, we barely scraped by most days.

Dad asked what we were talking about, and I briefly explained. "God has given us many privileges in this world," he said, now stirring stock. "Some people don't have anything. They have no health, no food, nothing. Do you think people with all those materialistic things you see on television are happy, Nisma? They're not. God does not give a soul more than it can bear."

I got up to help him serve the soup he'd made. "Well, Dad, when I have all those materialistic things, I'll let you know if that theory is correct. Until then, I don't agree."

He sighed as I set out the bowls on the table along with some bread. The rich scent of peppery soup pervaded the kitchen.

"Nisma," said Hannah as I took a slice of bread.

"My mum asked if it would be okay if we asked your mum and brothers to come and eat with us?"

I nearly choked on my food and quickly translated to Dad.

"You can try," Dad said, untying his apron and taking a seat. "But don't get upset if she tells you off."

"Let's go together," said Hannah. "I won't get offended, but Nisma, I'll need you to translate."

I gave a frustrated moan. I just wanted to eat, and I wasn't in the mood for Mum to bite my head off again. "I'm not in her good books. And I'm hungry."

"Bad luck," she said, and pulled me up by the hand. I was too surprised to stop her. "It's not fair you get shouted at all the time. I'll try and convince her all this trouble started because of us."

Mum and Dad's bedroom door was closed. I knocked twice before Mum called out in a tired voice, "Come in."

Asmar and Fadi were curled up on the sheets, their little chests rising and falling as they slept together, looking like dolls. Mum was on the edge of her bed, wiping her eyes with a tissue. I swallowed.

"Mum," I said quietly. "Hannah and Lilly would like to talk to you."

She looked offended at the very notion of it. "I don't want to see them," she whispered, anger in her hushed voice. "Or any of you."

Despite her tone, Lilly and Hannah followed me inside the cramped room. My parents' bed took up most of it, a curtain covering a nearby window. A woven rug, a brightly coloured mat my grandmother had made years ago, spread across the floor at my mother's feet.

Lilly sat at the edge of the bed, and I wondered if the woman had a death wish. Mum's face screwed up like she was going to vomit, and I was surprised she didn't shield the twins as though terrified Lilly would pounce on them. My shoulders tensed as I watched them, fully aware that Hannah and I were supposed to act as translators. At least with Asmar and Fadi sleeping, Mum might keep her voice down.

"Nisma, please tell your mother this," said Hannah, interpreting as her mother spoke quietly. "We're so sorry that all this tension has been brought to your family. We never meant to cause a rift or for Nisma to get into trouble at school. If I apologise from now until the end of time, I know you won't forgive me. That's okay because frankly, I never liked you either. But that was before I saw what a beautiful and passionate person you are.

You never complain about what you don't have, but rather, you're thankful for what you do have."

I interpreted as Mum sat with pursed lips, the whites of her eyes pink from crying. She didn't look angry, just defeated. It was somehow worse.

"For the first time in my life, I started seeing things differently. You're just a regular mother trying to hold her family together. I stopped seeing you as my enemy. You're not barbaric or anything we heard Palestinians to be. In other words, I learned to stop making assumptions. Your family took us in, however reluctantly, when my husband left me in the streets and long after our own family abandoned us. I understand now that race and religion is not the problem."

Hannah took a break while I translated into Arabic. The frown lines on my mother's forehead softened. We struggled with some of the English words – this was really pushing our skills – but managed to communicate well enough.

"Be the bigger person, Nada," said Hannah softly, echoing her mother's words. "Forgive me. For the sake of our children."

My heart bled for the woman before me, the woman whose husband beat her and had nowhere to go except a home where the mother of the family, a woman who could have been her friend, hated her because of her religion and where she was from. These were the words of a person who'd been broken wholly and completely. When I'd finished repeating her words in Arabic, Mum sat still without saying a word.

Her eyes travelled over me, then Lilly still sitting on the edge of the bed, then Hannah kneeling before her mother.

"Nisma," said Mum finally, and everyone straightened. "Tell these ladies I will never be their friend. Not now, not ever. What I have seen and been through in my life because of their people, they could never comprehend."

My stomach sank. What was wrong with her? Would nothing ever change her mind?

"However," she said as I opened my mouth, "what I can do is start treating them as my guests in this house, at least until they can find other arrangements."

Too tired to sugar-coat things, I told Hannah what she'd said. The disappointment on Hannah's face mirrored the misery I was feeling. Like me, she'd hoped our mothers could be friends. Lilly had certainly laid her heart out.

Leaving the boys sleeping, we headed to the

kitchen where Dad and Grandma were eating. Dad's eyebrows shot up when he saw Mum and he leapt to his feet, extending his arm to let her sit. I stared at him. Mum was always so sullen and angry and yet he loved her so much.

Mum's cheeks went pink as she gave him a playful slap. "Stop it, Salim! Don't be silly."

I remembered the story of how they met — how my dad had waited outside that little shop every day to talk to her — and my heart filled with admiration. I was lucky to have parents who loved each other no matter what. I giggled, and even Hannah and Lilly were grinning as we took our seats.

Dad, of course, tried to clear the air with playful conversation, talking about everything from clothes to makeup, and even discussing how to make the best soup. It was pretty good, too, and we all made sure to congratulate him on his culinary success.

The tension in Mum's shoulders eased, the atmosphere steadily clearing as we ate. Maybe one day, she and Lilly could be friends. I'd always hold onto that hope.

It wasn't until I was tucked in bed that I remembered
Dad and Grandma talking about Mum seeing the
doctor for tests. Was she really sick, or were they
just checking up on her? I'd forgotten to ask.

CHAPTER 7

About a week had passed since Mum's big blow up. Early morning sunlight shone through my window as strange sounds roused me from my slumber – hushed whispers and glass tapping on wood. I opened my eyes and Asmar and Fadi were there, right next to my bed, brown eyes wide as they stared at me.

"Gah!" I cried, leaping back in the sheets, heart pounding. "How many times have I told you both not to scare me like that? What do you want? Why are you up so early?"

They giggled and bolted from the room, baby feet slapping on the floorboards. Grimacing, I sat up, my nose filling with the strong chemical scent of...

"My nail polish!" I groaned, jumping out of bed. The little monkeys had opened three of my nail polish bottles, the bright liquid staining the floor. I snatched them up and put on the lids, but the lacquer had already seeped onto the wood in a glittery puddle.

I ran out of my room, screaming after my brothers.

"Mum!" I bellowed. "I'm going to kill your kids! *Muuuum!* Look what they did!"

"Stop that silly yelling, Nisma," said Grandma from the loungeroom. "Your mother isn't here. Your dad took her to the doctor this morning. She didn't sleep all night from the pain in her stomach."

That slowed me down. Anger still pounded through me as I stood breathing like a maddened bull, chest heaving. Those little monsters had run off somewhere and hidden. I wanted to spank them both with one of Dad's sandals. I went into the lounge where Grandma was sitting, looking as serene as ever, knitting. From behind her sofa, peeked the tops of two little heads.

"You can't hide them every time they demolish the house," I grumbled.

"I'm their grandma, Nisma, it's my job." Her wrinkled face broke into a smile. "A grandma protects twins from their evil big sister."

As though on cue, Asmar and Fadi leapt from behind the sofa. She put her knitting aside as they cuddled up onto her lap, laying their heads on her shoulders like perfect cherubs. I let out a frustrated growl and left to clean the mess from my floor before it stained.

After two hours scrubbing with nail polish remover and an old rag, the floor was looking close to normal. I heard the front door open and the low murmuring voices of my parents.

Mum's face was pale, dark circles beneath her eyes like she hadn't slept. To my shock, I noticed she'd been crying. Barely acknowledging me, she put down her bag and went straight to her bedroom, closing the door behind her. I swallowed and followed Dad to the lounge. Slumping into the lounge, he buried his face in his hands. There was silence. It scared me.

"Go play in your room, kids." Grandma shooed my brothers away and they scampered to their room. She set down her knitting and sat beside my dad.

"Salim, what's wrong? What did the doctor say?"

My heart seized in fear when Dad looked up, his eyes red from crying. Tears rolled down his face and into his beard. The air caught in my lungs and my chest heaved. A million thoughts raced through my mind. *Is Mum sick? Why's he crying? What's going on?*

I knelt before him as he composed himself, steadying his trembling fingers. "Nada, she…" his voice caught. "It's breast cancer."

The words hit me like bricks. *Breast cancer.* Sharp, ugly words that stabbed my heart. Fear flooded me as Grandma let out a gasp. It got worse when he kept talking.

"It's already spread to her spleen. An aggressive form, the doctor said. They—" he choked on his words, fresh tears pouring down his pink cheeks. "They can't do anything to help her, *Yamma.* They gave her a few weeks at the most. Her organs will start shutting down and she'll get more and more tired until there's nothing left."

Grandma gave a sympathetic groan, holding her son in her arms as the words blared in my head over and over like sirens. I shook my head. They'd made a mistake. This couldn't be my mother they were talking about. Sound became muffled as cold horror spread across my skin. *No, no, no. Not Mum.*

Grandma's voice pierced the bubble around my head. "Salim, does Nada know all of this?"

"She does, *Yamma*. She overheard the doctor telling me while she was getting dressed."

My legs gave way beneath me and I struggled to get up. My world was falling apart. *A few weeks?*

Lifting my head I looked straight into my father's eyes. "When did you do all these tests? How come you didn't tell me?" I could sense myself getting angrier and my voice louder. "How could you hide this from me, Dad?"

He paused for a moment, composing himself. "We only did the tests a week or so ago. Your mother did not want me to say anything before we had the results; she didn't want to scare you. The doctors themselves were not sure, Nisma." A single tear dropped from his left eye into his fluffy beard.

Asmar and Fadi had followed Mum to her and Dad's room. She held one twin on each of her legs, hugging them close as she sobbed, tears rolling down her cheeks. The boys were silent, comprehending that something was wrong but not knowing how to deal with it. She stroked their hair, hugging them close to her chest. She was so pale and thin – how had I not noticed before? Shame built up inside me. What sort of daughter was I?

"Let's go play, Mum," whined Fadi.

"It's not cuddle time yet," said his brother.

I gently untangled them from my mother's arms and ushered them outside to play.

"Nisma," said Mum as I sat beside her, draping my arm around her shoulders. "The doctor said I have cancer. I heard him telling your father. I… I don't have much time left."

Her tears dripped onto her clothes – wetting her shaking hands – as my heart broke. I felt numb. Tears didn't come. I hugged my mum tightly and put her head on my chest like she was a child. She sobbed into my dress; dazed shock spread through my limbs.

I wiped her tears away. This close, I could see the wrinkles around her eyes, the despair in those brown irises I knew so well. "It's okay, Mum," I whispered finally. "We'll go and see another doctor. Maybe this one doesn't know what he's doing and mixed up the results. Or couldn't read them properly."

It was our last, desperate hope.

"I'll tell Dad to find another one," I stammered.

"No, Nisma," Mum gave a rattling sigh, sitting up and wiping her cheeks. "This doctor is one of the best in the city. I had him reread the results three times. I'm not scared of dying." She cupped my face, and I wondered in that moment whether she'd felt this way ever since her first daughter had passed away. "In the end, we all die. But I'm so scared about leaving you and your brothers behind. They're still so young." Her voice broke again as a fresh tear dribbled down her cheek. "I will never see you get married. I'll never meet your children. Your brothers may not even remember who I am."

"They will, Mum."

"Who'll look after them when I'm gone?"

There was a sadness in her eyes I'd never seen before. I wish I had died and not lived to see her pain.

"You'll get better, Mum. Please don't think like that. Doctors get things wrong all the time," I babbled, laying her gently on the bed and pulling a blanket over her. "Just rest for now."

I kissed her forehead and left, closing the door behind me. My world had fallen apart. I made for my room, where Hannah and Lilly were waiting for me.

"What's wrong, Nisma?" asked Hannah. "We saw your dad and grandmother crying. Did something happen?"

"I don't want to talk right now," I said in broken English, feeling like I was wading through sludge as I passed them, seeking the refuge of my bedroom. "My mother… cancer. She's dying."

It was all I managed to say before I stumbled into my room, ignoring their gasps and their questions. I fell to my knees on the floor, near the nail polish stain my brothers had left. I'd been so angry. How was it this morning that *that* had felt like the worst thing in my life?

I trembled as anger built from the pit of my stomach and spread through my limbs like poison. How could this happen to us? There had to be a mistake. Mum was only 50 years old. She couldn't be dying.

I opened the thick cloth covering my window, blinking at the grey clouds that floated above. Birds twittered from the trees and voices murmured outside the café, like everything was fine and good in the world.

God, why are You doing this to my family? What have we done to deserve this punishment?

Finally, the tears came. I sniffled then sobbed, the

cries coming in short, ragged gasps as tears slipped down my cheeks and onto the floor, splashing the dark timber. I felt so helpless. There was nothing I could say or do to help my mother.

I looked up at a small patch of blue that had escaped the overcast sky. *God, I'm sorry. I didn't mean what I said to You. Please help me and my family. Don't take my mother away, please, for the sake of my little brothers. They're only three. Please, God. Please.*

I begged and prayed like a desperate child – on my knees, crying into my arms as I curled up on the floor. My head ached from crying. I must have sat there for hours, the sun slowly making its way across the sky and starting to set. Then came a soft knock at my door.

"Come in."

Dad's shoulders slumped, his eyes red from tears. He closed the door and sank onto my bed. When he spoke, his voice was dull, as though the life had been sapped from him.

"Nisma, my dear," he said, "I'd like you to help me make every day as comfortable and happy for your mother as possible. I don't want her to see us crying and miserable. If tears would cure her, I'd cry until the end of time."

His words made my eyes burn. I viciously wiped

at them as fresh tears pooled in my ducts.

"But all it would do is upset her. I want us to work as a team."

I nodded as I hugged him, burying my face in his chest like I was a child again. I felt so helpless. In that moment, I wished I was Asmar and Fadi's age, young and carefree.

"Dad," I said, my voice muffled against his shirt. "Why does God hate us?"

He stiffened. "Why would you say that, Nisma?"

"He's taking Mum away."

He gently cupped my chin and guided my face up until our eyes were level. It was terrible seeing my father so defeated. He sniffled, tears at the corners of his eyes. "Don't say that, Nisma. This is our trial in life, and everyone must go through trials. He doesn't hate us; He's testing us to see if we can handle this trial that He's putting us through. No matter how long a person lives, death comes knocking for us all eventually."

But Mum was only 50. It was far too soon. Just yesterday, we hadn't even known she was sick.

"Your mother will be going to a better place than this world," Dad sighed, stroking my hair. "Heaven is the ultimate hope for any human being that believes in the afterlife. I know that me telling you all this won't end the pain, but I want us to build happy memories while we can, as a family."

Happy memories. We had to try and make Mum's last few weeks on this earth happy ones.

"I've got something for you, Nisma." I shifted away from him as he took a small box from his pocket. "I was going to save it for when you finished school, but I think now's the time."

I took the box from his hand and prised it open. Inside was a little black phone. My eyes widened.

"Oh, Daddy," I said. "You… you shouldn't have. These are expensive, and—" My voice caught in my throat. I didn't want to think about doctors' bills.

"I've had it for six months," he smiled. "We were planning on surprising you with it when you finished school, but I'm giving it to you now. I want you to take as many pictures and videos of us all together as you can."

I nodded, carefully taking the phone and holding it like it was a precious gemstone.

"I want you to take as many pictures as you can and make a big canvas of us all together so I can hang it up in our bedroom," he said, his voice stronger now. "It'll be the first thing she sees when she wakes up and the last thing she sees before she sleeps."

I cleared my throat as sadness swirled in my chest. "Yes, Daddy, that'll make her happy." I wrapped my arms around him and held him close, inhaling his familiar smell. I was heartbroken for us both.

"I'll make dinner for all of us tonight," he smiled at me. "You help out with the twins and your grandmother and see if your mother needs anything."

"I will." I looked down at the phone in my hand. A camera for saving my mother's last moments, trying to capture happy times when we were already grieving. Just a day ago, if he'd given me a phone, I'd have been ecstatic, but now it meant nothing. I'd rather never have a phone if it meant Mum could be well again.

Dad left me alone. I allowed myself to shed a few more tears before braving the living room to check on the twins. I wondered if they understood what was happening – that our mother was dying – or if it had gone over their little heads.

They were sitting in Hannah and Lilly's laps, watching reruns of *Tom and Jerry*.

"Oh, Nisma," said Hannah as I collapsed onto the sofa beside her. "I'm so sorry to hear about your mother. I wish there was something we could do to help."

"Thanks," I said. My voice didn't sound like my own. Almost robotic. "But there's nothing any of us can do."

Lilly was quietly sobbing, holding Fadi to her chest as tears dribbled down her cheeks. I felt rubbed raw. All my emotions had been scrubbed away, leaving nothing but a shell behind.

"Hannah, please ask your mum not to cry when my mum's around," I whispered. "We don't want to upset her. Dad wants to make happy memories for all of us."

"Yes, of course. We understand." She nudged Lilly and whispered something in Hebrew. Lilly mumbled what I understood as an apology, wiping her cheeks and planting a watery kiss on Fadi's head.

"I'm going to check on my mother," I said, getting to my feet. A dull headache pounded in my temples. "Thanks for looking after the boys."

CHAPTER 8

I rapped on my parents' bedroom door.

"Come in," Mum mumbled.

She had just finished praying and was getting to her feet by the bed. Her dark hair was in a bun, several loose strands framed her pale face. "Nisma, come sit next to me, my child."

The room smelled like her. As I approached, I dug my fingernails into my arm so I wouldn't cry.

"Dad gave me the phone," I mumbled, not looking at her.

"He just told me," she smiled. "I hope you like it?"

"I do, Mum. Thank you."

"I have something for you as well," I sat on the bed as she shuffled to the wardrobe, extracting an old wooden box wrapped in muslin. She opened it carefully as I watched. Inside was a handful of faded photographs and a small necklace, the initials *A N* inside. Mum took the necklace and placed it gently into my palm, closing my fingers over it. Her hands were threadlike, delicate veins running like waterways under her skin.

"My mother gave this to me when I turned nine," Mum whispered. "She put our initials inside it. I wanted to give it to you on your wedding day..." her voice cracked. "But since I won't be there, I want you to have it now. One day, when you have a daughter and she gets married, please pass this necklace on to her."

I opened my hand to look at it. It was intricate, handmade. I could tell she'd taken good care of it. My heart ached.

Mum took the two photographs out of the box. One of them was a picture of a baby in a polka dot dress, sitting in a woman's lap. A man with a moustache stood beside them.

She looked much younger, almost unrecognisable, but I could tell by the shape of the eyes; the woman was *her*.

"This is your sister, Amal," said Mum, her finger tracing the grainy image. "I saved some money and took her to a photographer. She passed away a few days later."

Her words were heavy. Grief settled in my heart as I gazed at the photo. She was so tiny, far too small to have been taken away.

"When your brothers are older, I want you to tell them the story I told you about me," she said. "Let them know they had a sister named Amal."

I wiped my eyes as she reached for the other photograph. "This one," she smiled, showing me a picture of a handsome couple, "this is the only photo I have of my mother and father – your grandparents. I found it when I was staying at one of my uncle's houses and I've kept it ever since." The man had Mum's eyes, sloped and wide. The woman wore her hair in a braid.

There were tears streaming down her cheeks now, and I held the pictures in my hands like they were priceless treasures, my chest aching.

"I want you to show Asmar and Fadi this one as well," she said. "When they're old enough to understand. This is all I can give to you, my dear. I don't own anything else in the world."

I fought to stay calm, to stop the emotion welling up. "Don't say that, Mum. We don't want anything. Only you."

It took all my strength not to let the tears flow, my hands shaking as I took a deep, rattling breath. I hugged her tight, feeling her arms around me, inhaling her powdery smell and memorising it into my heart. She wiped away her tears, drawing back and looking into my eyes. I wanted to remember everything about her, committing every part of her face to memory so I'd never forget.

"Nisma, promise me you'll take care of the twins. Never let anyone else raise them except you and your father. Even when they become difficult teenagers, I want you to be like their mother and their friend. This is all I'm asking of you, my daughter."

"Of course, Mum," I whispered. "I'll look after them. They're my brothers, I would do anything for them."

She smiled and planted a warm kiss on my forehead. I wondered how she could smile at a time like this, when the whole world was crashing down around our ears.

The next two weeks passed in a blur. I didn't go back to school; I didn't see the point. I sort of floated around the house, cleaning and helping out where I could. I even cleared out our basement and scrubbed the staircase outside. Anything to distract me from my thoughts and watching my mother wither away. She took longer naps. The times she did spend out of her bedroom she just sat like a zombie, watching TV with her chest slowly rising and falling. She hardly ate – she wasn't hungry and whatever we brought her never tasted any good.

"Let's get ready for dinner," she said one breezy evening late in October. "No more tears. I want to use every breath that is left in me to build happy memories for us all."

She came out later in her best dress. She'd worn it when my brothers were born. She looked beautiful.

"Nisma, can you come and braid my hair for me?"

I blinked in shock. "Of course."

Mum *never* braided her hair. It was always in a bun or a bandana. My thoughts raced as I took her thinning hair, streaked with iron-grey, in my fingers and tied it into a neat plait.

"It looks wonderful," she said, admiring herself in the mirror. She looked like an entirely different person. "Can you pass me my red lipstick?"

She paused when she saw the surprise on my face. "Nisma, I don't want you all to remember my last days as a frail, sick lady who made everyone around her cry. I want to be remembered as the mother and wife who, until her last breath, built fun for her family."

She was trying so hard. My limbs ached like I was carrying the weight of the world on my back.

"At least let me fake a nice picture on the outside for everyone," she said, more quietly. "No one else can feel the pain in my body, and I don't want to inflict pain in your hearts."

She wiped away her tears with an old rag, carefully applying red lipstick. I'd never thought of my mother as a brave woman before, but what she was doing now showed a side of her I'd never seen. Respect mingled with grief as I forced a smile, nodding while she puckered her crimson lips at me.

We headed to the kitchen together, her dressed

like she was going to a party. Noisy chatter bubbled from inside – cutlery clattered while the stove sizzled and spattered. It was nice to hear mine and Hannah's family getting along – the four of them talking amongst themselves as they set the table.

"Hi Dad, we're all ready for dinner," I said as I paraded Mum into the room. One by one, they each fell silent. Grandma turned to hide her face, and I wondered if she was crying. Hannah's lip trembled.

"Oh, Nada, you look gorgeous today!" said Dad, slinging the tea towel over his shoulder. "You're looking younger than Nisma every day." He grinned and winked at me.

Mum's cheeks blushed pink as she took a seat at the table. "Nisma, darling, please bring your brothers in. I want them to sit next to me at the table."

I was about to fetch them when Asmar and Fadi burst into the kitchen, sheets tied to their backs.

"We're Superman!" they shouted, giggling. They squealed as I grabbed them around their waists and spun them round, like they were flying.

"Looks like the super *men* have arrived in town," I said, depositing them both on Mum's lap. They both hugged her tight as she held them, her eyes glassy.

"Time to eat, boys, before the food gets cold," she said as she settled the twins into their chairs, her voice steady.

Despite Dad's best efforts to bring cheer, melancholy hung over us in a dark cloud as we sat down to eat our falafel. Barely anyone ate anything. Lilly and Hannah sat in silence, poking at their food. It was a hard time for them, too. They mostly kept to the lounge, trying to stay out of everyone's way. I felt sorry for them, but there wasn't anything I could do about it. I smiled and they smiled back, Lilly reaching over to squeeze my hand. She looked so pitying I couldn't bear it.

"Salim," said Mum, looking pale. "Could you help me to my room? I feel tired."

She lifted the boys onto her lap, giving Fadi a kiss on his chubby cheek, then Asmar. My dad held her hand, guiding her to bed as we all sat staring.

"Hannah, shall we clear the table?" I said in English. No one was eating anyway.

"Of course."

Grandma put the boys to bed as we cleaned the dishes and mopped the floor. Dad reappeared, the jolly facade drained from his face.

"Nisma, leave that for now," he said, nodding at the mop in my hand. "Come sit with your mother.

She has a high temperature; I'd like her to see a doctor."

Fear spiked my chest as I hurried to Mum while Dad went to fetch the doctor. She was lying in bed, her breathing shallow. I touched her forehead; her skin burned beneath my fingers.

"Your father's so stubborn," she said weakly, smiling. "There's no need for a doctor."

"You're the stubborn one," I said softly. "You have a fever, and you've hardly eaten anything today."

Mum's smile faded as she locked eyes with me. "I feel my time is nearing, my child. What can a doctor do? Can he make me better, give me more time? It's a waste of money."

"Don't say that," I said, feeling useless. "He can give you some medicine to ease your pain and bring your temperature down."

I knew in my heart that what she said was the truth. No doctor would be able to help her.

"I want to tell you something, Nisma, before it's too late," she whispered, spilling cold fear down my spine. I was hit with a violent urge to flee the room, to run far away so I didn't have to see my mother like this; so I didn't have to hear her words, dripped with loss and grief. "I want you to forgive me for all my shortcomings. For not being the mother I should have been. I want you to never forget your promise to me that you'll look after the twins and your father when I'm gone."

I kissed her knuckles. "There's nothing to forgive, Mum. It's me who should ask you for forgiveness, for all the times I've upset you, for all the grief I've given you," my voice started to break, "...for thinking we had all the time in the world to one day become the best of friends." My tears finally defied me and exploded onto my face. I buried my head in her withering bosom, inhaling her warmth and smell – as if absorbing her would somehow stop her from dying.

Before I could say any more, the door opened and Dad walked in, the doctor trailing behind him. I moved out of the way, standing in the corner while he examined Mum. He was a slim man with large ears and a balding pate, which reminded me of an elf from *Harry Potter*. I watched in silence as he shone a torch in Mum's eyes, checking under her fingernails and beneath her tongue. He left the room with Dad without uttering a single word. I swallowed, my throat suddenly tight.

I sat beside Mum, watching as she closed her eyes, her chest slowly moving up and down. I pulled the doona up to her chin, her face pale and eyes sunken. She'd wiped off the lipstick, but her hair was still wrapped up in a braid, resting on the pillow. In the past few days alone, she seemed to have aged so much.

"Nisma," Dad whispered from the doorway. "Come outside, I need to talk to you."

Glancing at Mum one last time, I met Dad in the lounge, eager to know what the doctor had said. Grandma was there, sitting in her armchair. She looked strange without her knitting needles, her hands instead clasped together.

"It doesn't look good," he said, studying the floorboards. "She's in her last hours."

Grandma gasped, covering her mouth as her eyes filled with tears. My stomach plummeted. *No. No, it's far too soon.*

"There's nothing the doctor can do to help her. We just need to pray for now that Allah will ease her suffering. Nada's asked me to bury her, when the time comes, with her parents and her daughter."

Grandma was wiping at her tears. Shock filled me.

"But Dad, Mum hasn't been sick for long," I said, my voice shaking. "How can she have only a few hours left? Last week she was fine!" Anger rattled through me, a dark rage in the pit of my stomach that snaked its way through to my fingertips. "How can someone die from cancer just weeks after being diagnosed?"

Dad's face was blank as he looked up at me. "Nisma, your mum has had the cancer for a while, but we only discovered it recently. It's a rare and aggressive strain. Surgery won't help; the doctors are baffled that she hadn't shown any symptoms."

All the emotion poured out of me. I buried my face in my hands, my sobs coming in loud, ragged gasps, tears burning as thick mucus ran past my chin. Warm, strong arms enveloped me.

"Nisma, I'd do anything to help your mother, but I can't," he mumbled in my ear. "We have to be strong for her and the boys."

He wiped away my tears with his thumbs. "Let's get Asmar and Fadi. They can sleep with her tonight. She'll feel us with her."

Wiping my face with my sleeve, I followed Dad into the room where the boys slept.

CHAPTER 9

I sat on the bed and touched Mum's hand.

It was stone cold. Her chest wasn't moving.

"Dad," I murmured. "Mum's hand…"

Her face was white. Dad darted beside me and pressed his fingers against her neck, then lay his head on her chest. He stumbled to his feet and ran from the room, the door closing with a bang.

"Where's your father gone in such a hurry?" asked Grandma from the doorway. Hannah and Lilly were behind her, fear in their eyes.

I said nothing, too numb to speak as Grandma

checked for Mum's pulse, the colour draining from her face. In silence, she tucked Mum's hands under the blanket and covered her face with it. Lilly gasped as Hannah let out a dry sob. Grandma stood up, her back straight.

"To Allah we belong, and to Him we shall return," she said. "Nada is gone."

I didn't understand what she meant. *Gone?* I stared at her, then down to where the sheet had been placed over my mum's face. She wasn't moving, wasn't breathing. Deep down, I knew it. But in that moment, I was too numb to understand anything.

Everything blurred around me. Voices, people. Our neighbours appeared as Hannah and Lilly retreated to my room. The doctor was back, my father behind him, looking years older. An assistant of some sort accompanied them.

"Pronounced dead at 9:24 pm on the nineteenth of October 2017," the doctor announced in a hoarse voice. He signed a piece of paper and handed it to my father. "This is the burial slip," he murmured. "You need to give it to the cemetery."

Then he left without another word, as though he'd done it a million times today.

Dad pulled the blanket away from his wife's

body and held her. His crying was the most horrific thing I'd ever heard. He didn't sob, he wailed; he screamed and howled as he rocked my mother's lifeless form, clutching her tight. The dress she wore was soaked by the time he laid her back down.

I couldn't comfort him. There were no words for me to say. All I could do was watch. It felt surreal. I was in a movie – a tragedy void of a happy ending.

He wailed all through the night until, finally, Grandma gently pried him from my mum. "Salim, you must leave the room," she murmured in his ear. The day had broken – silver light escaping through the clouds and filtering through the bedroom window. "The ladies are here to prepare Nada for the burial."

It was like a punch in the gut. *Burial.* This was real.

I looked at my mother – eyes closed, braid still intact. She looked at peace, like she was sleeping. Except she'd never wake up.

Grandma held Dad's hand and gently escorted him from the room, him trailing behind her like a lost child. Two women I didn't know, maybe sent over by the doctor, came in with towels, a folded stretcher, and pieces of shroud that resembled a white bedsheet.

"We'll wash and shroud her now, dear," said

one of the women. She had soft eyes and a round face. "If you could wait outside?"

"I'd like to stay," I squeaked. Pity filled her gaze.

"All right, if you keep out of the way."

I sat in the far corner of the room on a stool, watching in silence as the ladies lifted my mother's body onto a stretcher. They undressed her and washed her body in a tub, an Islamic ritual for the deceased. As my bottom grew numb from the hard stool, I let the heavy, cold weight of reality settle in my chest like a stone, though the disbelief still lingered. I was waiting for one of the ladies to suddenly gasp, "there's been a mistake, your mum was just in a deep sleep!" Then Mum would wake up and smile at me.

She didn't.

They wrapped her body with the shroud, covering her from top to bottom five times. They left her face visible so we could say our final goodbyes. Then she'd be taken to the mosque so they could perform prayers and bury her.

"This is the last chance you'll get to sit with your mother," said the round-faced woman. She might have introduced herself, but I couldn't remember. "I'll give you five minutes, then I'll call the rest of your family in."

I nodded, shifting closer to where my mother now lay, still and wrapped, her eyes closed.

"I love you, Mum," I whispered, and the tears came, hot and fast. I didn't wipe them away; she couldn't see anymore. "I promise I'll never forget anything you taught me. I'll take care of the boys. Dad and Grandma, too. I love you so much, you will forever be in the depths of my heart. You are in a better place now. Until we meet again, I will always honour your memory."

I hugged her lifeless body for the last time and kissed her cold cheek. The bedroom door opened, and Dad walked in carrying the twins, my grandma behind him. Unaware of what had just happened, Asmar and Fadi continued with their playful jokes and giggles. It wasn't until Dad put them down that their eyes widened, trying to interpret the scene before them. I wondered if they even knew what 'dead' meant.

"Nisma," said Asmar as Fadi held my leg. "Why is Mummy sleeping?"

I looked to my dad for help. How do you tell a three-year-old that their mother is gone forever?

Dad scooped Fadi from around my leg and murmured to both of them, "Mummy's gone to heaven. We'll see her again one day."

Hannah and Lilly hovered at the doorway. I nodded to usher them in. Hannah hugged me tight, tears running down her pale cheeks. "Oh, Nisma. I'm so sorry. I wish there were something we could do to help."

"Thank you," I murmured.

Lilly hugged me too, her shoulders shaking with tears. She kissed my mother on the cheek then led Hannah out, leaving as quickly as they'd come.

The ladies covered my mother's face with a shroud and placed her on the stretcher. The men would take her to the mosque.

I watched from my bedroom window as they placed Mum into a makeshift coffin outside. I ignored the gasps and stares from neighbours and passing strangers, the murmurs of the obvious. I waved as they carried her away, a child waving goodbye to her mother.

I walked back to the lounge in a daze. The house felt empty without her.

I was met by a symphony of chattering voices,

mostly women, gossiping as though they were at a reunion party. If this was meant to be the first day of mourning, they certainly didn't seem sad. I didn't know most of them; we never really had visitors. Hannah and Lilly had made themselves scarce.

Grandma sat with two of my aunts. We hadn't seen them since Mum had the twins. Ignoring them, I retreated back to my room. I didn't want their sympathy. They were all two-faced cows anyway.

I hugged the pillow on my bed, my tears muted in the foam. *Why did this happen to us? What did we do to deserve this?*

My eyes fell on the items Mum had given me. I held her photos in my hand, gently stroking her face as my heart tore into pieces. I snatched up the phone, still sitting beside its box. I hadn't had a chance to take any pictures of Mum. Guilt and grief mingled into dark rage.

"Useless piece of junk!" I yelled, throwing the phone against the wall. What a waste of money. It was pointless now.

I hugged the picture of Mum close to my chest and closed my eyes, wishing that when I'd wake up, the pain would somehow be gone.

CHAPTER 10

When I opened my eyes, it was dark outside. I changed my clothes and silently opened my door, listening to see if the guests had gone. The house was silent.

I found Dad in the kitchen, slumped over the table and crying. It was horrible, seeing him sob, his hands in his hair as he blubbered, blinking red eyes.

I wrapped my arms around him and kissed his head. "Oh, Daddy. I already miss Mum so much."

He gently stroked my arm, his voice cracking as he croaked, "Me too, sweetheart. Today was the worst day of my life, Nisma. I buried the love of my life and a piece of my heart was buried with her. What'll we do without her?"

He looked up at me with those blue eyes I knew so well, and in that moment, it felt like I was the parent and he the child. "We'll get through this as a family, Dad," I said, though there was no strength in my voice. "Where are the boys?"

"They were crying for Mum, so Grandma took them to bed. They think she went to heaven to eat all the lilies."

I didn't know whether to smile or cry.

"I'd like to visit Mum's grave tomorrow, Dad. Hannah might come."

Dad looked up at me. "Nisma, you can't leave your grandmother alone to deal with all the ladies that are coming tomorrow to pay their respects."

I stepped back from him, my anger returning. "What ladies, Dad? I couldn't care less about them. Why didn't they ever visit Mum when she was well, or when she was sick, for that matter. Suddenly, they love her now? All they do is sit and gossip about each other. Mum always said, 'if a person doesn't see me when I'm well, I don't need their visit when the soil is on top of me'."

I expected Dad to argue, but he nodded, his face

hollowed with exhaustion. "Very well, Nisma. You can go in the morning, but don't stay long. You're to come back and help your grandma. I'm off to sleep in the boy's room. Goodnight, Nisma."

I swallowed, understanding. He couldn't face sleeping alone. "Goodnight, Daddy," I said, my voice quiet.

I didn't sleep for a moment that night, and instead sat on the balcony, listening to the sounds of insects and far-off rumblings of car engines. I thought about everything that had happened to us in the past month – Hannah, Lilly, Mr Yacoub… Mum – as the sun rose, bathing the world in light. When the clock told me it was nearly seven, I headed to the lounge and gently shook Hannah awake.

"Okay," she replied, her face scrunching with sleep. "Give me a few minutes."

She came to my room a little later, rubbing her eyes. "What's up?"

"Hannah, I'm going to visit my mum's grave. Will you come?"

"Now?" She blinked at my clock. "It's just gone seven."

"Dad said I have to be back early," I said, as panic clawed at my chest. I didn't want to go alone, not yet. I needed Hannah. "I want to be back before the twins wake up. Please."

I led her through the front door before she could protest. The cool breeze wafted through our hair and I shivered, wishing I'd brought a jacket. The sky was still pink with dawn, the streets quiet. Soon, children would be walking to school, some with their mothers. The thought made my stomach tie in knots.

I didn't have any money to buy flowers for Mum's grave, so I picked the best-looking daffodils I could find on the way, sticking out of the grassy gaps in the concrete. By the time we reached the cemetery, I had something resembling a bouquet in my hand.

An old man, the gravedigger perhaps, led us to where she'd been buried. My legs shook as we passed gravestones, some weathered by the years, others new and gleaming. A fresh grave sat beneath an oak tree. "This is it, my child," the man said.

"Thank you, sir."

Casting us a sympathetic nod, the old gravedigger

made his way back towards the entrance gate, leaving Hannah and I in silence. I knelt by the headstone.

HERE LIES NADA SHAHIN,
LOVING WIFE AND MOTHER.
11 FEBRUARY 1967 – 19 OCTOBER 2017.

I placed the daffodils on top of the grave and read some prayers while Hannah stood by the tree. When I broke down into tears, she was right beside me, quietly weeping as she entwined my fingers in hers.

I glanced around at the other graves. There were too many fresh ones, too many a result of bombs and war. All the greed and hate and killing – for what? No matter who or what we are, the earth is our final resting place. You don't take anything with you.

It turns out that regret is much stronger than gratitude in life. There was so much I hadn't said to my mother. She'd spent the last few weeks of her life angry and upset with me, disappointed that I hadn't listened to my teachers and may never get married. I hadn't made her as happy or proud as I could have. There was nothing I could do now except honour her memory.

Could my actions have led to her sickness? I didn't want to think about it. But, try as I might to push the thought away, it would always be there, niggling at the back of my mind – the possibility that I played a part in my mother's death.

I wiped at my wet cheeks and stood up, the cold air rippling my dress.

"I'll be *someone*, Mum," I promised, laying a hand on top of the cold stone. "I'll make you proud."

I turned to Hannah, forcing a smile. "Let's go home."

We turned and made our way through the cemetery, dry autumn leaves blowing around our ankles. Who knew what the future held for us. I hoped it would be better than what had passed.

CHAPTER 11

The days passed in a blur, the ache in my heart numbing as time went by. Eventually, I went back to school. It was pointless staying home crying all day. The boys needed me, and life had to continue.

Hannah and Lilly moved to the basement, insisting they couldn't be in the way any longer. I hunted for some spare blankets and pillows, wanting to make them as comfortable as possible. We barely used the basement. It was a stuffy, depressing place with a cold stone floor, brick walls and, since I'd cleared it out, not much else.

"Maybe we could bring some pictures down here and hang them," said Hannah with laboured cheer as she and her mother poked around the bare space. "Maybe a little desk for me to study."

Sobbing, I threw my arms around her. They were so brave. I could be brave, too.

"Come on, kiddies," I said to Asmar and Fadi as I got them ready for school the next day. I should've been nervous about going back, but at that moment, I didn't really care about Mr Yacoub or what the other kids might say. How could they hurt me after what had happened?

But Mr Yacoub, to my surprise, didn't take any notice of me at all. Most of the kids didn't either, though a lot of them seemed to suddenly stop talking when I entered the room. I didn't care. I'd get the best grades I could and make a new life. My family was counting on me.

I'd missed a lot of school, but I was smart. I could catch up. Mr Yacoub ignoring my existence suited me just fine.

I got home at the end of the day, throwing down my bag and collapsing onto the couch.

"Nisma, stop that silly throwing," Dad snapped at me from the kitchen. "If you rip your bag, I can't afford to get you a new one."

"Nice to see you, too," I said, annoyed. I'd just walked in and was already getting told off.

Asmar and Fadi suddenly ran through the lobby, chasing one another and screaming at the tops of their voices. Dad let out an angry growl.

"Stop that noise, you two! For goodness' sake!"

I jumped to my feet, scooping up my brothers, who giggled and yelled, flailing. Fadi's foot connected with my hip, making me gasp and drop him to the floor. Shocked, he burst into tears.

"You kids drive me crazy," Dad groaned, rubbing his face with dirt-stained hands. "Two erratic boys and a teenager. Not to mention the two women downstairs that I have to feed and pay for."

"Well, I'm sorry we're such a burden on you," I snapped, putting Asmar down and kneeling to comfort a sobbing Fadi. "I'm sorry I dropped you. Come on, twins, bath time."

When I came back, I found Dad thumbing through a small pile of cash, his face pale as he counted and laid out several worn notes.

"Dad?"

"What?"

I swallowed. He'd never snapped at me like this before.

"I was just thinking, I'm going to try harder at school from now on. I'd like to become a doctor after all."

He sighed, rubbing his face. His beard was tangled and overgrown and dark patches had started to form around his neck and at his armpits, like he hadn't changed his shirt in days. "Snap out of your bubble, child," he said finally. "You're living in an imaginary world. No one owes you anything. No one cares." My heart seized as his bloodshot eyes met mine. Tears began to sting in my eyes, but I blinked them away. "Life isn't fair." He held up the tattered notes in his hand. "It never was, and it never will be. It's survival of the fittest."

CHAPTER 12

——————————

"I'm going into the city today," said Lilly, kissing Hannah on the cheek. They'd spent over a week slumming it in the dingy basement now, and though Lilly spent most of her time scrubbing and dusting, it seemed they'd never escape the spiders. She was grateful to Nisma for keeping a roof over their heads, but they couldn't stay there forever. Now that America was off the table, she had to start thinking about how to provide an income for her daughter. She'd do any job she had to.

She watched Hannah and waved goodbye to her as she left for school. She and Nisma still walked separately, not wanting to provoke any more hassle from their neighbours or classmates. Lilly's heart bled for Nisma and her family. She and Nada had never seen eye to eye, but that didn't mean she didn't regret her death. She had been far too young and snatched from them far too quickly.

Lilly had gone to the city twice already looking for work, but today she'd spend the entire day in town. They needed money. Badly. They'd already overstayed their welcome in the Salim Shahin household, and now they were grieving. She'd beg if she had to.

She stepped outside into the cool November air, hoping that Hannah wouldn't have too much trouble at school. Maybe if she got a good enough job, she could move her to a new school for a fresh start. It was those thoughts that fuelled her determination.

Lilly hailed a taxi and clambered inside. "To the city centre, please."

She sighed, leaning back into the threadbare seat. An unfamiliar song – a little too loud for her liking – pumped from the radio. The driver ignored her, focusing on the road through slitted eyes. Lilly closed her eyes. First, she'd check the bakeries. She was quite good at cooking. If she had no luck there, maybe she could try getting a job as a seamstress or something similar –

Her eyes snapped open. They weren't heading for the city like she'd asked. They were bounding along a dirt road – bumpy and uneven beneath the taxi's tyres – surrounded by fields.

"Um, sir?" she asked, leaning forward. The driver didn't respond and the car suddenly lurched to a stop. From her seat, Lilly could see nothing but bushland and fields.

Nerves ate at her belly. "Sir, I asked to go to the city," she said clearly, wondering if the man could speak Hebrew. She didn't know how to say that in Arabic. "I'm—"

"Out, now," the man said gruffly, gesturing towards the door without looking at her.

"What?" she said, in a panic. There was nothing around here. She'd never get another taxi. "No, this isn't where I—"

"Get out now," he repeated, his voice so forceful that Lilly opened the door and scrambled out, terror clinging to her heart. Without asking for money, the taxi drove off, black smoke belching in its wake.

Now what?

"Hello, Lilly."

Her heart jumped to her throat as she swivelled around, coming face to face with a voice that she knew all too well. His hair almost reached his shoulders, and a thick layer of stubble coated his face, but there was no mistaking it, it was *him*.

Horror spread cold and fast through Lilly as she backed away, her hands covering her face. Her head still ached from where he'd hurt her in the past. As she met his cold eyes, her insides turned to water.

"Oh my God," she trembled, her eyes filling with tears. She looked around wildly, but there was no one else for miles. The taxi had left her in the dust.

"I bribed him to bring you out here," he said, a wicked grin painting his face as he approached her. He was several inches taller than her, his strides long and cool. Lilly looked around for anything she could use to defend herself, but came up short – the ground covered in nothing but piles of thin twigs.

"You still living with those filthy Muslims?" he asked, titling his head to the side. He was amused by her fear, it entertained him. "Still playing pet to those disgusting cockroaches?"

She whimpered as she backed into the road,

shaking her head. "Please, let me go," she said, her voice trembling. "Let me go and I won't say anything more about it. You need to find a new life."

"And let you continue to live yours?" he suddenly lurched towards her. She screamed, backing away from him. She tried to run, but his fingers closed around her ankle and she fell to the ground with a crash. The wind burst from her lungs as fists rained down on her chest. She gasped – palms bleeding – as he clambered on top of her.

"I'll teach you not to disrespect me!" he roared, delivering a stinging slap to her cheek. Burning pain exploded across her face as fingers – the same fingers that once promised to honour and cherish her for better or worse – wrapped around her throat. The same hand that she held as she defied her family's wishes to be with the man she loved clasped down tighter on her neck.

"No… please!" she tried to cry. The ground was hard beneath her. All she could see was his silhouette – the bright morning sun blinding her eyes. Weakness overcame her as she gasped for air, scrabbling to hurt him, to shock him into getting off her. But he was too strong, and her thin arms pushed feebly. His full weight pressed on her air pipe, and stars burst across her vision.

Sadness was the last emotion Lilly felt as the life left her body. She thought of Hannah, motherless and alone, of the mistakes she had made in abandoning her family, of her naivety in being tricked into his terrible trap. She regretted it all. Eventually, her lament turned black, and she fell limp.

He was panting, fingers still pressed into Lilly's throat as red bruises began to form on the soft flesh of her neck. Her eyes were closed, the shock frozen into her brow where dark hair stuck to her forehead. Her body was still. He sat back, crossing his arms over his knees, watching the trees gently sway in the autumn air.

Finally, he got to his feet, brushing the dirt from his pants. He'd waited half an hour for Lilly's taxi to show up.

He gathered his wife into his arms and threw her over his shoulder. Next was to get rid of the body. He knew just the spot.

He carried Lilly deeper into the bushes, letting her down within a cluster of pines. A shovel was already waiting for him. He started digging. Deeper and deeper he drove into the earth, coming closer to his wife's final resting place with every scoop of soil. With every hour that passed, the hole grew, until it was eventually deep enough to hold the woman's corpse. By the time he was patting the last shovel of soil over her body – perspiration sticking his shirt to his skin – the sun had started to set.

"Sir?"

Startled, he spun round. "Don't sneak up on me like that," he growled. "Is it done?"

His friend nodded. In his hand, a thick aluminium pistol hung at his side. "Over by the olive tree farm."

"Good work."

CHAPTER 13

Dinner had been a quiet affair. Grandma hardly said anything, silently sipping her soup. The twins had stopped asking why Mum wasn't joining us to eat anymore – they seemed to have gotten on with things better than any of us. Despite how little they were, they seemed to have grown up so much.

I glanced at Hannah, who was still waiting for Lilly to return from town. I hoped she'd come back with good news.

"I'm sure she'll find a job," I said to her as we

washed up. "She'll find something, something she *loves* doing. For a million shekels a week!"

Hannah giggled, though she seemed worried. It was already dark, and Lilly had missed dinner. As we sat studying in my room that night, I kept an ear out for the sound of a taxi pulling up at the house. But it never came.

At around midnight, Hannah went down to the basement to sleep and I turned off the lamp, wondering whether Dad had come home already. I was too tired to check. Pulling the covers up to my ears, I rolled onto my side. I'd just wait to see him in the morning.

I woke with a knot in my stomach. My head felt foggy, as bleak apprehension loomed over me like a storm cloud. I couldn't place it, but something didn't feel right. Something was off.

From my bed, I could hear chatter spilling through the front door. I cracked my door open to look.

Grandma shook her head as women babbled at

her from down on the street. "No, that's ridiculous," she finally snapped, shutting the door in their faces.

It was rare to see my grandmother angry. "Grandma?" I asked, stepping out. "What happened?"

"A ridiculous rumour," she replied, exhaustion weathering her face. We shuffled into the lobby, away from the muffled nattering of the women on the pavement, and sank into the sofa. "There's gossip up and down this street about your father and Lilly."

"What about them?" I asked blankly. The neighbours said foolish things all the time. We never usually took any notice. Grandma's eyes narrowed.

"That they eloped. Ran away together."

I almost choked on my spit. The accusation was laughable. There was *no way*.

But Grandma didn't look amused, her face sombre as stone.

"But..." confusion rippled through me. "Dad's at work. Isn't he?"

I hadn't heard him come home last night. I glanced at the clock; it was nearly time to get Asmar and Fadi up for school. Worry suddenly seized my heart. "Have you seen him this morning?"

"No..." she said slowly.

"Grandma?"

Fadi was at the doorway, rubbing his eyes. "What's for breakfast?"

"I'll get him," I said quickly, leaping to my feet and scooping him up in my arms. As I fed Fadi and woke Asmar, my thoughts stayed fixed on Dad. Had he stayed here last night? I checked his room, but the bed was neatly folded, no signs it had been slept in.

I padded down to the basement. Hannah was alone, still asleep. I shook her awake and relayed what Grandma had said.

I got stuck on the word 'eloped'.

"Um, it means to run away and get married," I said, and her face screwed up in disgust.

"Your father and my mother? No way."

I nodded vigorously in agreeance. Even if Lilly and my dad had spent any time together at all, which they hadn't, my mother had died barely a month ago. Dad would never do that.

"But she never came back last night," Hannah said, glancing at the mattress where Lilly usually slept. "All the way from the city…"

"Then let's find them," I said, getting to my feet.

"But what about school?"

I shook my head. "This is more important.

Come on."

We dressed and walked the boys to school, animated grins plastered across our faces. They already had so much on their plate; we didn't need to worry them about this too, not yet.

Internally, fear rattled through my chest. I could not shake the feeling that something was wrong, that Lilly and my father's disappearance was not a coincidence. I was scared to say it out loud – even to Hannah. I had no solid proof of anything yet.

After dropping the boys off, we headed straight for the olive fields. I tried to convince myself that my worrying was premature – that Dad had just been caught up at work and my fears were based on nothing other than my being dramatic. We'd walk up and see him there, underneath the olive trees, and everything would go back to normal.

Hannah trudged silently beside me the whole way, panic knitting her brows into one. Lilly had gone to the city alone, and anything could have happened to her.

Farmers and soldiers watched over the trees as usual. Harvest season would only last another few weeks, and soon they'd be tending the fields and looking for other work to tide them over until next autumn. Nobody took much notice of us until

I reached my father's small stretch of land, where two workers beat the trees and caught olives in their nets, ready to haul into crates. Neither one was my father.

"Excuse me. Has Salim Shahin been here today?" I asked, clinging to the hope that we'd somehow missed him.

"I'm sorry, he hasn't," said the nearest worker, a friendly-looking man named Hashem wearing a wide-brimmed hat to shield his eyes from the sun. "He should be, though. Remind him when you see him, will you? It isn't like him not to show up."

I gave a weak nod, feeling sick. So, Dad wasn't at home and he wasn't at work. Where could he be?

"What'll we do?" whispered Hannah. I glanced over the hill and clocked a group of Israeli soldiers clutching guns and staring at us.

"We'll get out of here," I said, quickly thanking Hashem and scurrying back the way we'd come.

Once we were out of sight, panic washed over me. Where was Dad? At the mosque, perhaps? But he wouldn't usually leave without saying anything, and surely not for this long.

I didn't believe for a moment that he'd left with Lilly. It was ridiculous. But my gut kept churning with the possibility that something had happened to both of them. Fear pummelled my insides.

I took Hannah's hand. Neither of us wanted to go home and sit around wondering, so we both went to school. Mr Yacoub barely acknowledged me as I sat down at my desk, excusing my tardiness under the ruse of a stomach ache.

I busily got to work, throwing myself into class as a way to distract myself from thoughts of Dad and Lilly. My final hope was that they'd be waiting at home when Hannah and I returned, with the best excuse of their lives.

They weren't, though. Grandma had been crying, not that she admitted it. After a forlorn dinner, Dad and Lilly's seats conspicuously empty, I took Hannah and Grandma to the lounge to talk to them. Translating between English and Arabic was difficult, but this was important.

"We have to tend Dad's olive trees while he's away," I said. "Otherwise, we have no income. I don't know where Dad and Lilly are, but we have to cover them until they're back. All right?"

I took Asmar and Fadi to school early the next morning, where a teacher kindly promised to take care of them until classes began. Then Hannah, Grandma and I traipsed over to Dad's olive trees. People gave us curious looks — two teenage girls and an old woman working the fields was certainly unconventional – but no one said anything as we harvested olives and packed them into crates.

"I'll get these," said Hashem near the end of the day, picking up the crates of fruit. We were sweat-soaked and exhausted. He pressed some money into my hand. "And be careful of the soldiers."

I nodded, storing the money in my pocket. Grandma sat nearby; I felt awful for pushing her.

"Grandma, stay at home tomorrow," I said to her that evening. "Hannah and I will tend to the fields and earn the money, and you can buy food and cook."

"What about your schooling, Nisma?"

"We'll study at night," I said firmly. I had it all figured out. If it wasn't so dangerous, Hannah and I could take turns going to pick the olives. We'd managed to dodge the soldiers so far, but I knew we were on borrowed time. I still remembered how scared I'd been when they'd come to bother Dad and I.

Working and studying was a good distraction, but when I lay in bed that night, worry washed through me. Dad had been missing for two days now. Should we tell someone? Would anyone try to find him?

The last thing I'd said to him – my sarcastic apology for being a burden on him – rumbled over and over in my mind.

Had we been a burden? Had he really run away? He was so angry at me – it was possible. *"Life isn't fair. It never was, and it never will be. It's survival of the fittest,"* he had said. His words, full of defeat, echoed in my thoughts.

I flexed my hands, calloused and scratched from the day's work. None of us had acknowledged how hard he worked for us. None of us had said thank you. I sobbed into my pillow, missing my mother, missing my father, wishing I could go back in time to when everything was normal, and hug them both close and never let go.

CHAPTER 14

We'd been working in the fields for two weeks. There was still no sign of Dad or Lilly and my whole body trembled with the possibilities of what had happened to them. I desperately hoped that they had run away together. It would be a hard pill to swallow, but I could deal with it — that they were alive and well, weathering the storm of judgement somewhere far away. They would return once it had all blown over. But the knot in my stomach told me otherwise — that they were gone and never coming back.

Harvest season was coming to an end and most of the trees had been stripped bare of their olives. I asked Dad's co-worker, a squat man named Khalil, what to do next.

"Excuse me?" I said, when he didn't answer me. Khalil was a quiet man, and often shifted away from us when we got close to him. I didn't know what his problem was, but Hashem had wandered off and we couldn't go home until we knew what to expect tomorrow. "Hello, sir? I asked you a question."

Khalil turned to me, and I was shocked to see that his eyes were red, like he'd been crying.

"I can't take this anymore," he wept. Hannah wandered to my side, and though she couldn't understand many of his words, she knew his tone. "I saw what happened, and I should have stopped it. But I was a coward."

"Stopped what?" I said, cold fear clenching my belly. I put down the net in my hands and took a careful step towards him. "Saw what, Khalil?"

He blinked at me, sorrow flooding his face as his dark eyes moved to Hannah. He spoke in a whisper. "Your mother…"

Hannah glanced at me. She understood "mother."

"She's… she's dead. They killed her and buried

her a half-mile from here."

The world around me spun; my legs buckling as bile rose in my throat. I fought to stay upright, swallowing the burning liquid back down into my stomach. "And my father?" I asked desperately.

"He's buried nearby. They killed them both. I'm so sorry."

Disbelief splashed down my back like ice-cold water. My worst fears had come true.

I suddenly had my fists around his collar. "What do you mean?" I yelled, so loudly that the surrounding workers turned to stare. I didn't care. Nothing mattered right now. "You're lying!" I cried.

"I'm not lying, Nisma. I'm so sorry."

"Where? When?" I felt like if the questions kept bubbling from my mouth, if I made as much noise as I could, then it would stop the painful truth reaching me – like I could chase it away with noise, with shouts of indignation.

"Tell me!" I screamed.

"It was a couple of weeks ago," he murmured. Perspiration beaded across his forehead, the smell of stale sweat permeating his clothes.

"Who did it?"

"I don't know – a man," he said. "He had a

beard, he was tall. That's all I know, I swear."

My fingers loosened on his shirt and he stepped back, swallowing. Hannah trembled beside me, her eyes frantically darting between us, unable to interpret what the man was saying.

"Your mother," I choked. "I… she…"

"Tell me," Hannah sobbed, grabbing my hands. "Tell me, Nisma!"

The world spun around me. "My father and your mother. Somebody killed them."

I was aware of feeling my knees hit the soil, of Hannah screaming at me. "Police," I finally managed to whisper. "Get the police!" And then I vomited all over the grass.

I don't know if I passed out or went into some sort of trance, but when I woke up, it was dark. The soldiers had melted away and a handful of police officers stood in their place, dressed in blue and clutching notebooks. Hannah sat nearby, her arms around her legs, rocking back and forth. Grief haunted her face.

I stumbled over to one of the officers who sat me down and told me everything.

Khalil had called the police not long after I fell unconscious, and it hadn't taken them long to find two shallow graves. They had concluded that Dad and Lilly had both been killed on the same day. He didn't want to tell me how they'd died.

"Let me see him," I choked.

"That's not a good idea," said the officer. "He's… not in the best way."

"I want to see him!" I cried. I had to see it to believe it.

Reluctantly, they led me to him.

Just out of sight from the fields, two long mounds, each draped in a dark sheet, came into view. Hannah's footsteps dragged behind me as I edged closer. I gave a curt nod, and the policeman lifted one of the sheets, exposing his face. I collapsed to my knees as grief caved in on me. It was my dad and Lilly, lying side by side.

I reeled back, bile burning in my throat. His skin was a sallow grey, damp with dirt where pieces of debris clung to it. He was maggot-eaten and rotting, but it was my father. They'd shot him in the head and buried him. There was a hole in his temple, crusted with brown, dried blood.

I sobbed, not wanting to touch him. *You were right, Dad. Only the strong can survive.*

The officer placed the sheet back over my father's face as I struggled to get the air into my lungs. The image of my poor, dead, maggot-eaten dad etched into my mind forever.

Hannah moaned nearby, the long painful sound of a wounded animal. They'd removed the sheet from her mother too, and a new agony, hot and sharp, pierced my heart as I saw the black bruises on her neck. Lilly's eyes were closed, her skin the same colourless, pallid shade as Dad's, her hair void of life and vibrancy.

How will their bodies be washed for burial? The wildly practical query flitted through the storm of thoughts in my mind.

Hannah crawled over and wrapped her arms around me, her body shaking in great, wracking heaves as she sobbed and screamed. I cried with her, the rush of people around us blurring as they covered their bodies and took them away. Still we knelt, sharing our pain, drowning together in an ocean of tears.

I couldn't utter the words to my grandmother. When the police told her, they asked her to sit down first.

"I'd prefer to stand," she said, knowing something was wrong as her blue eyes, so like my father's, darted from me to the men standing in her doorway. I trembled beside her as they said, in the gentlest words possible, that her son had been murdered.

"Our main suspect is Jacoub Cohen," said one police officer, and my grandmother's knees suddenly gave. Her breathing became harsh and ragged as I held her up from under the shoulders and helped her to the couch. It was like seeing a mountain crumble before my eyes. My once firm and unbreakable grandmother reduced to a weeping puddle. She didn't cry tears; they were a river, pouring from her eyes and pooling in her lap.

Why, God? I silently pleaded as my grandmother's heart shattered and her soul ripped to pieces. *What did I do to deserve this?*

That night, I wanted to die, too. "Take me and let me rest, already!" I hissed into the darkness. "Why are you keeping me alive in this cruel world?"

I opened my desk drawer to pull out our family

photo album. It looked worn, the once royal navy cover now pale and frayed. I had not opened it in years. A thick layer of dust coated my fingertips as I opened to the first page.

"They say a picture is worth a thousand words. Then a memory is worth a lifetime." My mother's words scrawled across the inside cover. I closed my eyes and ran my fingers along her handwriting, imagining her thin fingers holding the pen.

On the first page was a picture of me sitting in Dad's lap under an olive tree. I was all dressed up, wearing a white frilled dress and a flower through my hair. I would have been no older than three. Even in photos my father's face shone, his icy blue eyes leaking through the page. "Salim spent half an hour convincing Nisma not to rip the flower from her head just so I could take this photo."

I thumbed my dad's face, frozen in time, as tears pooled in my eyes. "I never got to tell you how much you meant to me, how proud I am to have you as my father. I hope I can raise the boys to have a big heart like yours. A heart that only ever showed compassion no matter what the circumstances were." Wiping my eyes, I kissed the photograph and closed the album. I could not handle seeing another picture. I felt my heart would stop.

CHAPTER 15

I woke before dawn and lay in the sheets, wide awake. I had thrown off the blanket during the night, the air unusually muggy and thick for winter. Making my way down the hallway to get some air, I found my grandmother sitting in the lounge beside an open window, tears streaming down her brown cheeks. She was in the same clothes that I had left her in the night before – it was obvious she had not slept yet. I didn't know what to say.

I shuffled over to her and placed my hands on her shoulders, gently massaging. She felt so fragile under my fingers, like she could snap at any moment. Like all of us, she'd lost weight.

"You know, Nisma," she sniffled. A gentle breeze caressed her grey curls as she turned to look at me, her eyes glittering with tears, the whites tinted pink. "The biggest test in this world is burying your own child while you are left behind to go on. When I had my children, I never in my life imagined having to bury one of them. It does not matter what type of child they grow up to be, being a parent never has an age limit. It doesn't expire.

"You know, your father was the closest to me out of all of my children. He was a brutally honest and very compassionate young boy, and this got him into a lot of trouble. When he was about your age, he befriended an Egyptian Jewish boy named Fadi." My eyebrows shot up in surprise. Dad had never mentioned this before.

"Your grandfather was furious! They constantly argued over this friendship. One day, Fadi went to sleep and never woke up. He had a heart attack and died at just 16 years old. Your father spent weeks and weeks crying – nothing we could say or do made a difference. Fadi was an only child and his dad had passed away when he was a baby. Years later, I found out that your dad used to go every day after work and see what help Fadi's mother needed, and get it done for her. He did this until her very last breath."

I reached to take her hand. The veins jutted from her skin like blue train tracks. "That's why he named my brother Fadi."

She looked up at me with the same ocean eyes of my father and nodded. "How am I going to live the rest of my days without him?"

Dad's body was taken to be buried properly beside Mum's. Like before, neighbours who usually ignored us decided to show up, and no matter where I went, I couldn't escape their whispers. Still they were convinced that Dad and Lilly had had an affair. Even Dad's brothers – who had all but abandoned him after he chose to wed my mother – were here.

Fury built in me at their hushed voices – at the way the wives and grandmothers abruptly stopped talking when I neared them. The words 'affair', 'elope', and 'dirty Jews' floated on the air and I caught them.

Then I suffocated them.

"That's it!" I cried, slamming down a tray of dates. "Everybody out! I won't have you disrespecting my father like this!"

Shocked silence. The guests stared back at me – some wide-eyed, others shaking their heads in disapproval.

"I said *out!*" I roared, barely registering my grandmother's arm hugging my shoulders. I blinked back tears as our guests filed out, muttering their criticisms. They were just here for the free food anyway. No one cared about my father.

No one cared about any of us.

I could no longer control the anger inside of me. I leapt around the room, smashing a dozen glass cups onto the floor. I threw the plastic chairs into the walls, and the food at the windows. Everything in my sight I hit, and bashed, and broke. The house was destroyed, and so was I.

I fell to the floor crying, my head in between my hands. I just wanted to die.

Later that night, once the graveyard fell quiet, I knelt beside the fresh stone engraved with my father's date of birth and death. There it was, right next to my mother's, beneath the oak tree. I laid down the flowers I'd picked on the way, running my hands along their gravestones as hot tears bubbled in my lids. Now I was here, I could finally feel it. Emotion crashed into me like tumbling waves, and soon I was sobbing.

"You left me alone to the wolves," I whispered. "How can I stand up now?" My murmurs became screams. "You can't both go and leave us behind! What about the boys? Grandma? Me? Why? Why didn't you take me with you?

"Please, I'm not strong enough for this!" I collapsed to my knees, tears dropping like bombs onto the grass.

"Did you do this to punish me? For taking in Lilly and Hannah? I have learnt my lesson! I would give up one hundred Zionists if it would bring you back, Dad." My desperation dripped with venom, "You were right Mum! Standing up for what you believe in is only a privilege for the rich, not the poor. Nothing good came from taking in those settlers. They killed your dad, and now they've killed mine."

CHAPTER 16

I hadn't spoken to Hannah in days. Down in the basement, she slept all day, refusing to talk to anyone, not that I'd tried particularly hard to rouse her. Though I had calmed down after my outburst at the graveyard, I wasn't ready to continue on like we were best friends. Not yet, anyway. I certainly didn't blame Hannah for what had happened, and during moments of clarity I felt painfully guilty for my wicked thoughts that it was her and her mother's fault that my dad was dead. But, every time a wave of grief washed over me, hot blame rose from my gut and choked me like bile. I couldn't be a true friend to Hannah while my mind remained so volatile.

Grandma had tried to coax her out with food, but she didn't want to eat. All she could do was lay in her grief. "Hannah isn't well," Grandma said. "Without any money or family, there's not much she can do. The police have made arrangements for her mother's body. They'll give her a Jewish burial, I suppose."

As bad as I felt for Hannah, there was no room in my heart left for sympathy. Somebody had murdered them both. Someone had stolen them from us.

Grandma forgot to cook most days, so after school I'd make dinner – my soups and stews nothing compared to my mother's. It was all a waste, anyway; no one wanted to eat. Somehow, Fadi and Asmar knew Dad wasn't coming home.

I was so exhausted I could barely move, shuffling despondently from one task to another. I washed and cooked mechanically, like a robot that barely functioned. No money. No will to live.

One breezy morning, I woke up to knocking on the door. I opened it to find Khalil on the step, his eyes red from crying, his shoulders slumped with grief.

"Here," he said, sniffling as he handed over an envelope. "I'm so sorry I didn't tell you sooner. I was… scared."

I stared at him, too numb to understand what he meant, too grief-stricken for manners.

"There's money inside," he explained. "Me and the men at the olive fields collected some together. It should keep your family tied over for a couple of months while…" his voice trailed off as he sighed. "Good luck, Nisma."

I visited the police station every day after that. They said they were gathering information on who may have shot my father, but it didn't seem like anything was being done.

"We think it may have been a Sharaf case," said Officer Odeh, a man with heavy-lidded eyes and broad shoulders. "An honour killing. We have several suspects."

"Well, who are they?" I demanded.

Officer Odeh's eyes narrowed. "We can't discuss that with you, young lady. Why don't you run on home? Shouldn't you be at school?"

School was feeling less important by the day, but I'd made a promise. My dad wanted me to be a doctor. Every spare moment that I wasn't studying, I followed Dad's and Lilly's investigations.

The same person had killed them; that was obvious. Whether it was a Sharaf case or not, the person or people who'd done it needed to be punished.

"I wish I could erase his genes from me," Hannah said tearfully that night as we studied by candlelight. She looked gaunt, her skin sallow where it hung beneath bulging lids. Her once lustrous hair was now thin and dull. Over the past week, I had managed to convince Hannah to leave the basement and join me for dinner and study. I wasn't sure that it was helping her. "I hate him. It was him, I know it."

I put down my pen, not meeting her eyes. I knew it was him, too. Hannah's father. He had the motive to kill them both. But we didn't know where he was, and with each passing day, it seemed the police cared less and less.

"I swear if I ever see him again, I'll kill him myself," said Hannah through clenched teeth, the pen in her fingers quivering as she clutched it with whitening knuckles.

I felt powerless. There was nothing either of us could do. Who cared about the plight of two young women in this unfair world?

CHAPTER 17

The weekend rolled around, and when Grandma promised to look after the boys, I visited the cemetery again.

Dad's grave was still horribly new and fresh, the earth ballooning above where his corpse lay.

It still didn't feel real. I kept expecting him to appear over the hillside, a smile on his lips, ready to greet the day with hope like he always had. I didn't realise it until now, but I was more like my mother, cynical and angry. The only difference was, she'd been strong, too.

"I swear I'll get to the bottom of this," I muttered into the darkness. "They won't get away with it." But, deep down I knew my promise was hollow. In a country like ours, justice was seldom served.

I visited the station again the following day. A mean-faced officer with a name badge reading El Masry frowned up at me, sighing like I was a pest.

"You need to stop coming here," he said, putting down his pen. Papers were strewn across his desk and his thick black eyebrows reminded me of hairy caterpillars. "The investigation is over."

"What?" I asked, my insides turning to water. "What do you mean, *over*?"

"Not enough evidence," he said, picking up his pen and signalling me to leave. I stood my ground, fists clenched.

He looked up at me again, his expression softening. "Save your breath, my child. Look after yourself and your loved ones. You won't get anywhere with this."

I backed into the wall, my hand trembling as

I pointed at him. "You've accepted to be silenced out of fear," I spat. "But I won't back down!"

I was hauled outside by two waiting officers who threw me onto the pavement like a bag of garbage. Frustration pounded through my veins as I kicked at the dust. *Useless, all of them!*

They'd been bribed; I was sure of it. I sobbed all the way home, hating this life and this world.

"Grandma," I said as I entered the lounge. The boys were asleep on the couch, their cheeks pink from tears, their little chests rising and falling. Grandma was knitting, stiffening as she looked up. I knelt before her, taking her fragile hand in mine.

"I'm going to become a doctor," I said. "Dad always wanted me to. I'll work the fields in the mornings and at the weekends, and I'll study at school in the afternoon. I'll work hard for a scholarship and make you all proud, I promise."

Grandma hugged me. She felt so thin, like she'd snap if I held on too tight. "I am proud of you, Nisma," she whispered. "I'll do better, too. I'll buy groceries and take care of the boys. You've been so brave."

I fell into a routine, and it helped with the grieving. I got up early each morning to tend the fields, trimming back the trees and clearing the grass around them. Khalil and Hashem helped me find other jobs to tide me through the off-season – working the land of nearby citrus and vegetable farmers and performing other odd jobs around town. It was hard at first, but my muscles soon grew seasoned with strength. After a quick lunch at home with my grandmother, I went to school and studied. Mr Yacoub's silence evolved into one word answers, and eventually short sentences. It seemed he was torn between his hatred of my defiance and his sympathy for me losing both parents. I didn't need his pity, just his tutelage.

Hannah and I worked hard, studying in all the free time we had and often late into the night. We had some catching up to do, but many kids our age didn't go to school full time and had gaps in their knowledge. With us attending classes every afternoon and studying hard at night, we found we caught up to the others quite quickly. Eventually, we reached the top of our classes. Though I was exhausted, I was learning. I'd become a doctor one day.

I exercised in my spare time to make my body

strong. I wouldn't be weak. I wore jeans and shirts – any clothes I could find at the market, not caring if they were meant for boys. Maybe in another life I'd have been considered attractive. Maybe I'd even have married young like my mother always wanted. But there were many things my mother wanted that never came to fruition.

Hannah and I kept to ourselves – we didn't have time to make friends. The other kids thought we were strange because of our cold words and aloof stares, but their snipes and sneers no longer bothered us. What did things like schoolyard gossip, courting and parties matter when we'd both lost our parents, when we'd experienced firsthand the unfairness that gripped the world?

Our pain had hardened us to stone, and our only hope was to make something of ourselves. We refused to be swallowed by the trauma and corruption that plagued our country – that had taken my parents and Lilly. We could not accept the hand we had been dealt; we needed to break the cycle of poverty, suffering and violence. I may have lost hope of ever living a happy life myself, but I'd never lose hope for my family, or for the people of Palestine. For as long as the blood of the olive tree ran through my veins, I would remain strong and steadfast, as unremitting as that rugged plant.

After months of gruelling work, it turned out to be worth it.

"Hannah! It came." I flew through the house in a flurry, the letter flapping from my hand like a child's rattle.

"Nisma!" she squealed. We had been waiting on high alert for this for weeks. Finally, we would find out if everything we had gone through – all of our sacrifices, labour and perseverance – could save us. The thin manilla envelope held the fate of not only me, but of the entire family.

I slipped my finger under the seal, carefully slicing it open.

"Dear Ms Shahin," I read aloud, "We are pleased to offer you a scholarship to the University of Qu'laif, commencing Semester 1, 2019. Congratulations! Please complete the enclosed documents to finalise payment. We look forward to seeing you in the fall." I leapt across to Hannah, bear hugging her shoulders as we jumped up and down.

It wasn't a top tier institution by any stretch, but any dreams of studying abroad had been left in shambles after my parents' deaths. I could still become a doctor this way, and I'd be a fool to turn down paid tuition.

I saved up money to buy things for school, excitement for my future pulsing through my veins. I'd become a doctor; the best doctor Palestine had ever seen!

EPILOGUE

"I graduated," I said to their gravestones. Though it had been years, I still visited every week. The flowers I'd brought last time were slowly drying, their petals starting to blow away in the wind. "I fulfilled my promise to you, Dad. I'll be a doctor, just like you always dreamt I would be." I blinked back the tears that threatened to fall. "I promise both of you that you'll be proud of me from now on."

I was proud of Hannah, too. Even though we came from different backgrounds and believed different things, she was my sister now. Family was not only blood, but those who were with you through the bad and the good.

We were moving on. Maybe one day, we would heal.

"Sometimes I try to smile when my brothers are around," I said to Hannah one night as we ate dinner. Asmar and Fadi were studying in the lounge, a habit we'd encouraged them to pick up. They had grown so much over the last six years – their stocky toddler bodies having melted away to reveal the wiry frames of two young men. They had endured so much loss in their short lives. It was up to Hannah and I to shield them from any more suffering.

"We're so broken that men could never understand," said Hannah. She'd hardened to stone, like me, and I couldn't remember the last time I'd heard her laugh. Her long hair was pulled back in a tight ponytail, dark strands about her face as she ate. "To love someone, you have to have something to give them. What do we have to give? Dead parents? A family to take care of? No money?" She grunted through her nose, dipping bread into her soup. "A dead future?"

I stared at my friend's face. There was no life in it anymore. Would we ever heal from our nightmare? Would our small successes make up for the sad mess that was our lives and fill the crevices in our hearts where our parents used to be?

I wanted to answer her, but what could I possibly say? Instead, we just sat together, comforted by the other's presence. Her thin arms wrapped around me as I relaxed into her chest. Neither of us had to say anything more. Sometimes, silence made more noise than the loudest scream.

Dad was right – life isn't fair. All we can do is our best with what is given to us. It is up to us to rise and resist that which tries to bury us. Hannah and I had resolved to keep moving, to do better. And that's what we were going to continue to do.

The Nisma from six years ago was gone – she had died with my parents. I knew now that my teenage optimism had been naïve. I was foolish to have thought that if we could all 'just get along' that the unfairness in the world would dissipate, that corruption, inequality, poverty and death was a by-product of simple adult stubbornness. It was much, much more than that. The horrors of this world were insidious, and no 16-year-old child could have changed that alone. The world didn't owe me anything.

However, as broken as life had left me, I still had hope. Not for me, or for Hannah, but for Asmar and Fadi, for their children, and for the generation after that. I had to believe that our sacrifices would add to the ripple of change toward eventual peace for the people of Palestine. For as long as there were Jews and Arabs willing to judge one another independent of race or religion – like Hannah and I had – we would eventually repair our violently fractured reality. One day we would be free.

As I lay in bed that evening, I looked at the pictures my mother had given to me, now framed and arranged on my desk alongside my textbooks. I saw the grandparents I'd never met, my sister and mother smiling. I liked to believe they were watching over us, protecting us.

Asmar and Fadi knocked on my bedroom door, edging it open, their two little heads poking through the crack. "Nisma, we can't sleep," whispered Fadi, his eyes red and strained. "Would you tell us a story?" Asmar yawned, his slender arms bound around an old, worn toy.

"Okay, monkeys, but then it's back to bed. You have school tomorrow."

"Yes, Nisma." They shuffled in, curling up at the end of the bed.

"Okay. Ready? I'm going to tell you the tale of the strong and brave Princess Nada, and how she overcame all of life's hurdles to find true happiness."

Fadi's eyes opened wide, the corners of his mouth twisting into a smile. "She has the same name as Mummy!"

"That's right, monkey," I smiled, poking the end of his nose.

My thoughts often wandered back to the promises I had made our mother – to protect the twins, to tell them of her life before us. When I closed my eyes, I could still see her sitting next to me at the end of her bed, her powdery scent washing over me as she gave up the only possessions she had ever owned. Now seemed as good a time as any to fulfill the simpler of her two requests. "Snuggle in, and I'll tell you the story."

I took my brothers through the details of our mother's life, laced with childhood fantasies of kings and queens, kingdoms and dragons. I told them about Amal. About our grandparents. About

Maria and how Dad had gallantly swept Mum off her feet. The twins grinned from ear to ear, clutching at my waist.

"There is something I want to show you," I said as I reached the story's end, shimmying from their grip and shuffling over to the desk. "See this picture?" I picked up the wooden frame, handing it to them. "This is her. Your sister, Amal."

Asmar and Fadi gazed at the portrait of the baby in the polka dot dress in the lap of our mother. They studied it thoughtfully, taking turns examining the baby's tiny features, her face so like Mum's. I hoped they weren't too young to understand, that they'd be able to accept our mother's past – that learning it would make them feel closer to her.

"She has the same eyes as Mummy," said Fadi eventually, his head dipped. "Nisma," he continued, peering up through thick black lashes, "do you think that the princess is happy now?"

"I do," I replied, patting his head. "She and Knight Salim are watching down on us from their kingdom in the sky. Princess Nada has finally been reunited with her King and Queen and precious baby Amal. She has finally found peace in *Jannah*."

The twins smiled up at me, their little heads glowing with adoration. They were so strong.

Despite everything they had been through, they somehow remained cheerful. It gave me faith. Maybe one day I would smile again, too.

I had no idea what our futures would hold, but I knew we would never stop fighting for more. We would not bow to the wind, no matter how hard it blew.

We were unbreakable. We were strong, and we were resilient. Just like the olive tree.

It seemed like I finally understood its story.

ABOUT THE AUTHOR

Mariam El Houli is an author, entrepreneur, and loving wife and mother. Of proud Lebanese background, Mariam lives in Melbourne, Australia with her husband and five children. Mariam obtained a Bachelor of Literature and Composition from Griffith University.

Mariam created global skincare business, Eve's Skin, from absolutely nothing. Vegan, organic, and Australian made, Eve's Skin offers premium skincare at affordable prices. She also co-founded Mica Minerals, an organic mineral makeup brand.

When Mariam isn't penning her next bestseller, heading her prosperous skincare label, or doting on her family, you can find her whipping up delicious Lebanese delicacies in the kitchen.

Mariam's aim is to save the world one book at a time.

www.mariamelhouli.com

COMING SOON
Adult fiction

Saving the world one book at a time.
Mariam El Houli writes for humanity with
one fierce intent: to take cultural and social
taboos and reveal their forbidden secrets on paper.
She illuminates the complexity of human relationships,
social dynamics and cultural entanglements, capturing
the best and worst of humanity.

Her gripping debut adult fiction *Souls of the Devil:
Grey Wolves* is a breathless page-turner set to shock and
surprise at every turn. The finely constructive narrative
set on the coast of the Black Sea in northeast Turkey is
jam-packed with drama, telling an unforgettable tale of
regal family bonds, betrayal, greed, lust and love.

To pre-order your copy, go to mariamelhouli.com